Cat's
MEOW

Dale Mayer

CAT'S MEOW: BROKEN PROTOCOLS 1
Beverly Dale Mayer
Valley Publishing Ltd.

Copyright © 2014

ISBN-13: 978-1-773363-85-1
Print Edition

About This Book

After a year of hell, Lani Summerland's life is just getting better when she's tossed unceremoniously a few hundred years into the future with her orange Persian cat, Charming Marvin, in her arms. With no way to fight it, no way to go back, things are only looking to get worse fast.

Breaking protocol is cause for severe consequences in the time and world Liev Blackburn lives. But, after a year of government regulation, the crackdown is easing up and he begins to relax. Everything he's worked for is hinged on keeping his reckless brother in check. But, while he's been protecting Milo from falling under the government's ever-vigilant radar, his brother has been working on a surprise present for him, one that's the cat's meow… Lani is that gift—a woman from the past that Liev has been fixated on.

Milo never anticipated having his brother's dream girl come to their time with a snarky cat that can not only talk but doesn't have a clue how or when to shut up!

Books in This Series:

Cat's Meow

Cat's Pajamas

Cat's Cradle

Cat's Claus

Broken Protocols 1-4

Sign up to be notified of all Dale's releases here!

https://geni.us/DaleNews

Protocol 1:3:1. You will in no way use technology to damage the life of another— particularly if those actions are to selfishly enhance your own.

CHAPTER 1

LANI SUMMERLAND WAS on top of the world. It had taken several years, but she'd finally put her past behind her. A new day had begun. A new job, her first date in a long … okay, in a very long … time, and, for once, her future looked bright.

It had been the years of hell, especially this last one.

She glanced at her plain black watch and realized, after working later, she was running a little behind. She wanted time to prepare for her date. She'd actually hoped to have a lot of time to prepare, but her boss hadn't been easy to deal with today and insisted she complete some work before leaving. Normally it wasn't a problem, but today was special. Only she was new to her job and didn't dare do anything but what was asked of her with a bright smile.

As soon as she completed the job, she'd logged off and bolted out of the building. She walked faster on the busy street, her head bent against the wind and the rain that threatened. Rush hour had peaked, but plenty of people still raced to get home. Equally focused on their destination as she was. Her apartment was just a few blocks around the corner.

For the umpteenth time, she pulled the faded, crumpled photo of her and Lawrence from her pocket. He'd been everything to her. Now, one year after her very public humiliation, she could finally say she'd recovered. She was at a crossroads in her life. A good one. A place she'd worked to reach for the year. But she'd made it. Now it was time to get rid of the picture. She'd hung on to it as a reminder. Of a painful lesson learned, to never be forgotten. Some rules were never meant to be broken—and ignorance was not an excuse. She'd had some inkling that things with Lawrence weren't as they'd seemed, but young love and all the rest of those glorious emotions, guaranteed to get her into hot water, had overruled her better judgment.

So she'd ignored those little nudges. Until she had found him at a company event, as the host, in fact— with his beautiful young wife at his side.

That had been the most disastrous evening of Lani's life. The wife's mocking look and laughing comment to Lani later in the ladies' room about being her husband's latest side piece hadn't helped. That the woman knew had been bad enough but from her words, it was obvious she and her husband had laughed about her. Just the knife twisting in the wound. The pink slip from his legal firm the next day was just another insult and another piece of her education.

Never have an affair with the boss—especially when it turns out he's married.

She'd been such a fool. She hated that the other

staff had known—and no one had said anything to her. That they all believed she was the kind to have affairs with married men. Now she got those snide comments she hadn't understood at first. The mocking and disgusted looks she hadn't connected to the truth. Too bad someone hadn't blurted out something to clarify the situation. It might have been painful and humiliating at the time, but she'd have put a stop to the affair immediately.

Nothing like learning about men, life, and consequences the hard way.

A garbage can was up ahead. She stopped, carefully ripped up the picture—one that she'd once loved and held dear—into tiny pieces and fed them slowly into the can. She smiled, feeling a wonderful sense of freedom as each piece disappeared from sight.

Then she turned, pulled up her coat collar, and raced the last few blocks home.

Time to let go and to create a better future. And, as of today, it looked damn bright.

"WHAT THE HELL?" Liev studied the massive wall of monitors in front of him. The computers should all be locked behind the security field at this point. He glanced around the large empty office to see if anyone had slipped in behind him, but he was alone in the encroaching darkness. Then again, he should be. It was damn late, and it was his brother's office. No one was allowed in but the two of them. Not in this age of computer espionage. His world lived on computers, and his brother was a genius when it came to programming. There was nothing he couldn't create.

Hence the large company that they started together, with a few family backers, and the heavy security measures they used to keep their inventions secure until their official release. Some were not meant to be released. Ever. If it weren't for Milo's recent odd behavior, that little-kid look of having a secret he desperately wanted to share, Liev wouldn't be here now. Genius Milo—chocolate-munching, green-mohawked, geeky Milo—had been acting suspicious for days.

That would give anyone nightmares.

As Milo's business partner and older brother, and company CEO, Liev didn't dare let Milo go off half-cocked again. Genius he might be, but he lacked a certain level of common sense, as proven by the slap from the Commonwealth Council Protocols Association (CCPA) special Regulatory Commission Group last year. And their intensified monitoring of Milo thereafter. No one doubted Milo's intentions—just that they weren't clearly thought out. At the end of the nerve-racking CCPA review, the board had determined that the brothers would be allowed to continue their IT company, but the genius needed to be carefully watched.

A year later, the regulatory overseeing eye had

eased—slightly. But the scrutiny had chafed for both Milo and Liev. For Milo more so.

And, as Liev stared at the complex coding on the screens mounted in the center of the wall, he realized that Milo was in deeper than before. But what was he creating? And how much trouble was it going to bring them all? Liev's heart sank. This last year had done nothing to smarten Milo up. This program looked to be almost complete, if not ready for testing. But Liev knew nothing about it. And why was that?

"I wondered how long it would take you to check up on me." Milo's quiet voice spoke from behind Liev.

Liev dropped his head into his hands, wanting to pull his hair out. Instead, he said in a low worried voice, "What have you done?"

"It's nothing bad. In fact"—Milo's voice picked up enthusiastically—"it's kind of awesome."

"Kind of awesome?" Liev spun around to glare at his kid brother who didn't know when to quit. "This could mean jail time. You know that." He towered over his younger brother. "This could mean losing the company. Years of our time and effort. Years where the family helped us, backed us, protected us. Did you even think of that? Did you once think about the consequences? About what will happen to me? Or does any of that matter?"

"No. No, it doesn't." Milo rushed over, wringing his hands. At least the childish delight of the last few days had dimmed. Milo just didn't get that rules and regulations were there for a reason. Liev did. He lived by them. His brother didn't even acknowledge them. And Liev had been bailing Milo out since he was a little boy—he wouldn't change now.

Milo loved history. And, when he added in his crazy geek skills and a complete lack of comprehension of the limits to what he could do, all manner of hell could happen. Had happened. Was possibly about to happen again.

"You don't understand." Milo beamed with excitement. "See? It works this time."

Liev shook his head, not mistaking his brother's meaning. He was talking about the same damn project that had gotten them into trouble last time. "No. It doesn't."

"Yes." Milo hopped from one foot to the other. Passion and joy were on his face and in his voice. "It does. It does. Honest."

"There is no way. You can't just go back in time and yank a person forward a couple centuries into our world. Look at what kind of trouble that got you in last time." Got us, but he kept that bit quiet. Milo's enthusiasm got him—them—in trouble every time. But, every once in a while, Milo came up with something so earth-shattering that most people had no trouble overlooking the problems that came with Milo. Then again, they weren't the ones having to clean up after him.

Milo walked over to the keyboard, his fingers dancing so fast that Liev could barely follow what he did on the screen. Colors and figures flashed at alarming speeds on the massive wall of monitors in front of them.

Liev might not be the creative genius that Milo was, but he still knew more than most about coding. "Hey, stop. You can't test this right now."

"Sure I can. It works. I actually planned to test it tonight anyway. I just didn't expect to have you here. Having you here though … it's perfect."

Raising both hands in frustration, Liev gave an exasperated snort. "You were hoping that I wouldn't be here. Right?"

Milo shot him a resentful look. "You never let me have any fun."

"Fun?" Liev said ominously. "Going back in time, snagging up any female you want, and dropping them into our time is fun? You do remember what happened last time, right?" His glare deepened. "The massive power outage you caused?"

"I figured out how to stop the massive power surge. Besides, I only wanted to brainstorm with Marie Curie," he said resentfully. "She was an intelligent woman. We'd have had a great time."

"If you didn't kill her in the process," Liev snapped.

Milo spun around to face him, his grin once again splitting his face. "No, I fixed that. It's safe now."

"Says you." Liev eyed his brother suspiciously. He didn't know how to get this into his brother's head. This was too important. "This is big. Like *seriously* big

stuff. And the chances of you doing this successfully ...
You know the protocols are very specifi—"

"Ah, but the protocols are poorly written." His elf-ish grin flashed, and he added, "Besides, they are more like guidelines."

Milo nudged his brother to the side. "You might want to get out of the way."

"What? What for?" Liev spun around and caught sight of Milo reaching for a button on the side. "No. Stop." And he knocked his hand away. Milo stumbled backward, tripped, and fell against his keyboard. The screen went nuts as Milo's elbow smacked the button anyway.

Immediately a high-pitched whine filled the room. Liev slapped his hands over his ears, even as his eyes stared in panic at the monitors dancing with flashing computer code.

"What's happening?"

"Everything!" Milo danced, laughing like a loon. "But it's nothing to worry about. It's supposed to be like this."

A flash of light exploded in the center of the room, blinding them both.

CHAPTER 2

L
ANI GLANCED AT the clock, realizing she had just
enough time for a cup of tea and a snack before
getting dressed. She filled her teakettle and placed it on
the stove. Her trip home in the brisk weather had left
her chilled inside. The tea would help. The snack would
take the edge off her hunger until she was served
dinner. She smiled, wondering what restaurant her new
beau was taking her to.

She danced a quick jig across the living room. Perfect day, perfect date, and a perfect evening to come. If
she had any misgivings that her bubble was about to
burst, it had to be residual negativity left over from the
years from hell. And maybe a twinge of a reminder that
Murphy's Law had been formulated specifically with
her in mind.

But that was over. She was all about new begin-
nings. And that meant she could open the bottle of
wine she'd been saving for a special occasion. Screw tea.
Wine would warm her up too. She reached into the
back of the fridge and pulled it out. Twisting the top
off, she poured herself a glass and held it up to sniff it.

Charming Marvin, her overgrown orange Persian

cat, jumped lightly onto the counter. She bumped the wineglass gently against his nose.

"Cheers!"

Meow!

Lani flipped her long blond braid behind her back and laughed. "Right back at you, big guy. Here's to us." Eyes closed, she took a large gulp of her wine. Still too buoyed to relax, she put her glass down and snagged Charming up. Humming a tune in her head, she twirled him around.

"We're gonna be just fine."

Meow!

She laughed and twirled him again. She wanted to enjoy this moment. It had been a long time coming, but it was all good. She felt fine. In fact, she felt better than fine. She felt great!

Her life was back on track. It had been a long, painful struggle, but she'd made it.

Tonight would be good too. Danny was a cute single guy who had transferred into the company last month. Life was good again. Joy filled her heart. It had been a long time since she'd felt this way. She glanced down at her cat, and said, "You know what I've been through, don't you?"

Meow!

"I wish you could talk, Charming. Just think how great that would be." She did a quick pirouette with him. Just as she slowed down, a white light exploded in her living room.

Invisible waves blasted her, picking her up and throwing her against the couch, Charming clutched fiercely in her arms, his claws digging deep into her skin, a strange howl ripping from his throat. Mist swam through her brain, and her eyes burned. Her chest squeezed tight. She couldn't breathe. Her ears rang, and her lunch was crawling up the inside of her throat. She tried to cry out but no words came out.

What the hell had just happened? She could only hope the property damage would be minimal. Otherwise her landlord would freak.

She had to get out of here. If that had been an earthquake it could happen again. If it had been some kind of accident then fire could be next. She didn't dare stay inside. Besides, her lungs were screaming for fresh air.

She sat forward, clutching Charming tightly, afraid he'd take off, and that she wouldn't be able to find him again. Moving slowly, her muscles heavy and unwieldy, her body in major shock, she struggled to her feet and headed for the doorway. Smoke filled her living room. She stifled a cough and covered her mouth with her sleeve to avoid breathing the reeking aroma.

She crouched low, gasping for air.

Had there been a gas leak? A bombing?

Then she heard voices. Oh, thank God. She struggled toward them.

A strange voice cried out, "Damn it, Milo. What did you do?"

"Wowza." A cackle filled the air. "Look. It worked!"

Through the mist, she spied two men, ... or, at least, she thought they were men. The one in a purple and turquoise skintight suit with a green mohawk bounced in front of her, a maniacal laugh coming from his mouth. Then her shocked gaze landed on the second man.

Lawrence?

And that couldn't be.

Her heart slammed against her ribs, and then she really couldn't breathe. She gulped for air as she stared at the one man she'd loved and hated—and had spent the last year trying to forget—who now stood in front of her. Staring at her—was it possible—equally shocked?

Unbelievably, after all this time, her anger rose in a red haze. She stepped into his personal space and smacked him—hard.

His head flipped to the side, then came back around slowly, a red mark quickly rising on his cheek. Shock lit the deep dark depths of his eyes.

Uh-oh.

She took a step back, her ribs frozen and locked.

He took a step forward.

Finally her lungs expanded. She took a deep breath, spun around, and ran.

She raced out the door and headed toward the elevator. And somehow got turned around. There were no walls of elevators. Nothing looked right. ... Nothing looked normal. What the hell … Blindly she ran from door to door, until she found one leading outside and bolted through.

And came to a skittering stop. Her mind couldn't process what her eyes saw. She was on a balcony—a very high up balcony. And that couldn't be either. Her apartment was on the third floor, whereas, from the scenic panorama laid out before her, she had to be at least sixty floors up—if that was even possible. There were no buildings in her town even a third that tall.

The view in front of her was like nothing she'd ever seen before. It appeared to be a city. Or rather a metropolis on steroids. Buildings rose in weird space-agey-looking domes, and railcars raced along big circular runs. And—God help her—vehicles flew high above her head.

It looked nothing like Vancouver, BC, where she lived. In fact, as she shuddered and leaned against the closed door behind her, this didn't even look like her planet.

"WHERE DID SHE go?" Milo cried out. He spun around and said, "She's gone."

And damned if he didn't look like he would cry. Liev dropped his hand from his cheek only to raise his hands in irritation and snapped, "What did you expect? You snatched her from her world and dumped her here.

She panicked and ran. Of course, she did. We have to find her."

"Find her? Where else can she go?" Milo dashed up beside Liev. "She can't go anywhere. That's the beauty of this."

Liev spun on his heels to stare at him in shock. "Really? I think you forgot to tell her that." Exasperated, Liev raced out of his brother's design room and into the short hallway. There weren't many places for the woman—and whatever she clutched in her arm—to go. This was an office building, thankfully at nighttime. The security system was on and most of the offices would be locked up tight. Several more doors were ahead, and he could only hope she'd gone in a straight line. Actually, he could hope that this disaster was just a bad dream, but knowing his brother ...

"We have to stop her before she finds a way outside." To lose her in that jungle would be a tragedy. And he had had enough of those on his hands with this damn technology as it was. If the government got wind of Milo's latest experiment, Milo and Liev could both be thrown in jail and their technology confiscated, never to see the light of day—unless those in power wanted to use it for themselves.

And that would be disastrous.

The ruling governmental Council had too much power now. Dealing with them was worse than dealing with the CCPA. Much worse. Who knew what the Council would do with something like this technology?

Knowing how corrupt the Council was—it would be nothing good.

Liev couldn't believe Milo had finally succeeded with his time-travel project. His kid brother was a genius like none other, sure, ... but to do something like this? ... Liev kept moving forward and opened every door he came to and still found nothing. He raced for the front door, his heart sinking. Please don't be outside. Please ...

"Wait—"

Too late. Liev had already barreled ahead and made it outside before his brother's words infiltrated his frustration. "Okay, this is bad," Liev said. As he watched, the line of buildings in front of him slowly went dark, one after the other. Just like last time. "So very bad."

"I didn't do that," Milo said when he caught up to his brother. He held up his new SXC4500 fingerboard computer and shouted. "I have her on the camera."

Liev spun around. "Where is she?"

"She came back inside." Milo flipped the comp around so Liev could see.

"Really?" That stopped Liev in his tracks. He peered at the screen. "That was actually a really smart move."

Milo grinned. "Yeah. See? I didn't choose a bimbo. We need someone with enough brains to handle this type of switch in her life."

"That's not measured by brains. So much more is involved here."

"Oops," Milo said, looking back at the screen. "She's on the move."

Milo's new rocker boots clicked as he raced behind Liev back into the facility. Liev shook his head. Milo needed a keeper himself. How could he possibly determine the type of woman who would not go crazy from his damn experiment? Anyone would be completely freaked out by such a trip. And what about her physical state? That she was on her feet and moving was incredible. That she appeared to be cognizant enough to be searching for a way out was ... well, that was beyond belief. And fit right into the scope of Milo's unbelievable success. Regardless of the poor woman's health and emotional or cognitive state, Milo had pulled this female from wherever she'd been living happily, and he'd somehow dumped her in his office.

Still blown away, the two brothers retraced their steps as they tracked her through the building. Minutes later they ended up back in Milo's office with still no sign of her.

"She's in here somewhere," Milo muttered while clicking away on the tracker. "The tracker is operating erratically. I'm struggling to lock onto her position."

Liev searched behind the chairs and under the desks. "Please tell me that you can send her back." Liev turned to his brother. "That you can reverse this process."

"I don't think so." Milo threw him a sideways grin. "Besides, we don't want to send her back."

"I do," Liev snapped. "And I'm sure she wants to go back too. She has a life. Remember?"

"*Hmmm.* According to my research, Lani Summerland doesn't have much of one." He clicked through his fingerboard computer and read off the list. "No partner. No career to speak of. Failed business after one year. Managed to stay gainfully employed. No marriage. No children. No long-term friends on record."

Chapter 3

THEY KNEW HER name. Lani sank lower in the empty closet she'd hidden in as the painful litany of her failed life washed over her. She buried her face against Charming's fur, her arms tightening until he protested. Only his voice was hoarse and weak. Then she wasn't feeling all that great either. That kid's words weren't helping. What a horrible dissection of her years to date. Surely it hadn't been that bad? Besides, it's not as if her life was over. She could achieve greatness yet. Couldn't she?

"It's not that simple, Milo."

Lani heard the discussion despite the noise of doors being opened and closed. The kid's name was Milo? And what was his relationship to Lawrence? Her mind spun on endless questions as she struggled to sort out where she was and how she got here.

The deeper of the two voices spoke again. "She has reasons for what happened in her life. Sure, she *might* be up for a move a couple centuries into the future. She *might* consider it an adventure. She *might* consider it an improvement on her old world. But you didn't ask her. You didn't give her a choice, and that makes all the difference. You just yanked her out of her old life. For all you know, she might have a major plan about to come to fruition, and you stole that from her."

"I did not," Milo protested. "I did my research, Liev. I'm not an idiot. She had nothing. She was nothing. She would have become nothing. Now she is something—special."

Her heart squeezing tight, Lani listened to Liev— not Lawrence—and Milo discuss her life. As if they knew her. As if they knew everything about her. And she meant *everything*. How was that possible? And then came the big question of why? Why her?

"And where in her psych profile, Milo, did it say she'd be up for a complete shock like this?"

"Ahh ..." Milo stuttered.

Liev's voice dropped to an ominous level. "You didn't get a psych profile, did you?"

"Well, it's not so easy. They didn't do them regular-ly back then. They were quite primitive people. Remember? Those types of analysis only happened with people that were unstable."

Liev snorted.

Lani's chest locked tight. A couple centuries into the future? They were kidding—right? But, from what she'd seen outside, before instinct had her spinning around and returning to the one space she knew—this room—she was not in Vancouver, British Columbia. At least not Vancouver as she'd known it. And she'd lived there all her life. Her city was gone. Her apartment building was gone. Her living room was gone. She was alive but her life as she'd known it was … gone.

She squeezed Charming tighter against her chest and buried her face against his thick orange fur. Thank heavens he was safe with her. The two of them could have gotten blown up in the blast. "You're all I have left," she whispered. And got the next biggest shock of her life.

"Hey. What do you mean *all?*" Charming said, twisting in her arms, his paw reaching out to bat her chin. "You make it sound like I'm nothing. And I'm a whole lot more than nothing."

Lani reared back and stared into her beloved cat's glowering eyes. She shuddered and closed her eyes briefly. Maybe she had a head wound? A concussion, she thought hopefully. That would explain the crazy phenomena. Immediately, she felt better. Until her gaze landed on her cat.

"Charming?" she asked cautiously. "Is that you talking?"

No, it can't be. How stupid. She shouldn't even have asked that question. It had slipped out instinctively. No way her cat could talk. Then again, no way could she have been yanked two centuries into the future either. She dropped her head back. She was losing it. Tears gathered in her eyes. Why her? All she'd ever wanted was to be happy. Was that so much to ask for?

Questions rippled through her mind. Terrifying her. Making her heart stall, then race like she was being chased. She squeezed her eyes shut again. One tear rolled down her cheek. She turned her head to wipe her face on her sleeve. She needed some normality here. Something real she could grab and hang on to. She took a deep breath and whispered, "Please, Charming, don't tell me you can talk."

And, oh, God, … he actually answered her.

In a deep voice, unlike anything she'd ever heard before, Charming said, "I could always talk. Since when did you learn?"

She swallowed, opened her eyes, and stared at her best friend. And found him staring at her, his face only inches from hers, with a puzzled look in his eyes. Such a human look in that gaze. Such a human-sounding voice. And words … English words. Strung into normal sentences.

Except the claws in her flesh were all feline.

Her mouth dropped open, and she shook her head in denial. "Not possible. It's not possible. It's. Not. Possible."

"Well, it's possible but it's not *probable*. I figured you were too primitive, too underdeveloped to learn such a skill." He brightened, that wide mouth twisting up into a grin. "But you surprised me. You actually learned to talk."

At last she understood.

She was crazy.

She'd finally turned some invisible corner into a complete fantasy world in her mind. She'd always wanted to talk to animals. It had been a secret dream ever since she had been a little girl. Obviously reality had become too much, and she'd retreated to her childhood state. It was almost a relief in a way. To have an explanation for this insanity.

It was either that or she was having a crazy dream. And that was all too possible. Not to mention being a better option.

She beamed at her cat. "I'll wake up soon, and this will be just a happy memory."

"I wish I was dreaming." Charming snorted. "This little room is nice and cozy and all, but where is the couch? Or your bed? A big fluffy pillow? I need my nap."

"Sleep? You need to sleep?" She shook her head, staring around the tiny closet. "I was getting ready for a date."

"Yeah, great." Charming gave a jaw-splitting yawn before tucking into her shoulder. "Who needs a date? Well, okay, you do, but really I need my beauty sleep." And he closed his eyes.

She stared at her cat and whispered, "Please let this be a bad dream. And please let me wake up soon and find everything back to normal."

"I hope so," Charming muttered, "because you forgot to feed me dinner before we time-traveled."

At the words *time-traveled*, she forgot to breathe again. When she finally got oxygen back into her lungs, she cried out, "Don't say that."

Suddenly the closet door opened. The same two men peered in, but the green mohawk, so large and long, was all she could focus on.

A scream caught in the back of her throat. But no sound came out.

"Aha. There you are," said the owner of the mohawk, Milo, if she'd gotten the names right. "And who were you talking to?"

She wanted to fight. Wanted to kick them both in the teeth so hard they'd never eat again. The older one, Liev—or at least more staid and adult looking male of the two according to what she'd seen and heard, even though he was the spitting image of her nemesis—peered around the green hair. This close, she could see he looked very similar to Lawrence, but something was younger, cleaner about his features. And maybe nicer. Lawrence had gained a seedy look to his cheeks and a perpetual smirk to his eyes.

As if he was always one up on you.

Which, in her case, he had been. And, if Liev wasn't Lawrence, she had just smacked a complete stranger for no good reason.

Damn.

She risked a look at Charming, saw the feline smirk as if to say, *Uh-oh, now you're in trouble,* and she shuddered. In a low voice, she said to Charming, "You can bite them in the balls while I run."

"Not happening." And damn if her cat's voice didn't drop low to match hers.

Liev reached down, grabbed her elbow, and yanked her to her feet. She tugged her arm back, climbing out of her hiding spot on her own, holding Charming protectively away from him. She shot him a dark look. "You don't have to hurt me."

He retreated instantly, his hands out in front of him apologetically. "Look. I'm sorry. We won't hurt you. Please. Let's sit down, and we'll explain everything."

She raised one eyebrow and proceeded to repeat everything she'd heard them say. Their eyebrows shot up. She added, "As you can tell, I can hear just fine. Now I want you to tell me how the hell you'll fix this." She glared at Milo. "I want to go home."

Milo jumped forward, his face earnest and proud at the same time. His eyes glowed with excitement. "See? That's the thing. We can't. That's the beauty of this technology. It can't be reversed."

"And that's beautiful?" she asked ominously, her heart and mind screaming their protests in sync. "How do you figure?"

While she waited for that explanation, she realized the men were guiding her into a glass cube she hadn't noticed in the dark room. She could barely see her surroundings, but the room looked like a futuristic office with huge wall screens she'd never seen before. And some kind of center console. The wall screens looked see-through and had all those weird colors. She couldn't tell what was outside that wall from her current position inside the cube. With *them* joining her.

Once inside, she sank into the deepest corner to avoid their touch, holding Charming tight. He was her one link to normalcy. He stared up at her and opened his mouth.

She slapped a hand over it and glared at him. And realized that, if Charming could talk—there was nothing *normal* left.

Trying to process the situation faster, she studied the men with her and Charming, waiting for something to happen. Liev pushed something on his wrist, and the cube took off. She shrieked, reaching out a hand instinctively to steady herself, only to find the ride smooth and quiet.

She couldn't help but be reminded of the old *Charlie and the Chocolate Factory* story with the glass elevator that seemed to travel outside of buildings. Except this wasn't likely to have as happy an ending as that story did. As the glass cube swept around corners, she noted it wasn't on rails. In fact, it didn't appear to be attached to anything. She gasped and squeezed her eyes closed. "Where did the ground go?" she whispered.

"It's there. Below us."

She peeked through her eyelashes to see the bottom of the glass cube and nothing else. Just a swirling whiteness—as if they were in the middle of a cloud. Her arms clutched Charming reflexively. Her mind spun, grasping for any reasonable explanation—and came up empty. She fell against the glass cube, hyperventilating. "Oh, this is not good. This is so not good."

Milo explained, "It's just a modern elevator."

That didn't deserve a response. There was no *just* about it. His idea of a modern elevator and hers were miles apart. She shifted Charming in her grasp but dared not loosen her hold. Not that she had any chance of dropping him with his claws dug into her arms. She wouldn't be surprised if he'd drawn blood. If so, she'd be dripping blood onto their glass floor.

The elevator changed directions again, sending her lurching sideways. Oh, shit. Oh, shit. *Oh, shit.* She felt the beads of sweat rise on her forehead.

"It'll be fine," Milo said with a wide grin. "We're perfectly safe."

At the end of his words, the glass box came to a complete stop. And it dissolved around them. As in, here one minute and gone the next. She slowly straightened wondering how it was she hadn't fallen backwards. But there'd been support right up to the end.

The men exited—if there was a cube to exit. They'd barely traveled. It almost looked like the same building—or maybe the same set of buildings? There'd been no sign of the outside world at all.

She straightened, took one step in their direction, and, without warning, her stomach heaved and the effort landed her on her butt.

"OH, YUCKY. THAT'S so … yucky." Milo danced away

from her, his face a picture of morbid fascination. "I'm calling someone to clean that up."

"Fine, but let's not be here when they arrive." Liev knelt by the woman's side, trying to ignore the reek from the mess at his feet. Sweat had beaded on Lani's forehead—at least that's the name he thought Milo had called her—and her color had gone a pasty gray. Her breathing had turned shallow and irregular. Probably a delayed reaction. Rushing forward a couple hundred years had to be tough on the stomach, if not the rest of her. That she could even walk and talk and ... look half as sexy as she did was amazing. And he shouldn't be noticing. Now she'd curled into a small ball, her slim frame rocking back and forth. The massive furry critter in her arms made a horrific howling sound that set Liev's nerves on edge. He might have sympathy for her, but that animal ...

Through the noise, he heard her whispering into the animal's fur, "It's okay, Charming. It'll be okay, baby."

"I know it's hard to believe, but you are right. It will be okay," Liev said, hoping he wasn't lying to the poor woman, "but there is no way I can agree with you calling that ... that thing *baby*."

And damn if that furry thing didn't rear back and glare at him. As if it heard and understood.

Lani froze, lifted her head to stare at Liev, and then she did something that completely disarmed him.

She started to giggle.

CHAPTER 4

L ANI COULDN'T STOP giggling. She tried, but her laughter came in never-ending waves. It was more stress relief than hilarity. She had to stop. If she didn't, her out of control glee would turn into tears soon. And that would be bad news. For everyone.

"Oh, brother. What an ass," said Charming in that low guttural whisper. "You can pass on this Lawrence too."

Her laughter rolled out freely. She caught sight of the two men and the combined shocked looks on their faces. They might have managed to toss her forward a couple hundred years, but she'd managed to shock them. And she planned on keeping them off-balance.

She had to find a way home, and she needed their help. But she'd be damned if she'd let them walk all over her. Knowing what was outside the building scared her shitless, and, for all she'd been trying to shake off her old life, she hadn't meant to shake it off this far.

And who was this Liev? With each glance to confirm that Liev looked so similar to Lawrence, she had to consider he'd come forward in time as well. But she had discerned just enough visual differences too. Then again, she hadn't seen Lawrence in over a year. That could account for some of the differences in his appearance. She stole another look in his direction. No, Liev was younger. Much younger. Besides, how likely was it that the two of them were dragged forward in time? And, if they had, were others like her here? She perked up at that idea. If there was a group them, maybe they had a way to go home too.

"It's not the same guy," Charming muttered.

She wiped the tears from her eyes as her laughing spell ended and holding Charming so the men couldn't see her talking to him, whispered, "Why do you say that?"

"Because you're in the future. That means he's not the same man." He shot her a look of disgust, adding, "Duh!"

She pursed her lips at the sarcasm, not even close to being able to digest Charming's new communication abilities or indeed the sarcastic responses that seemed to roll off his tongue and, stared up at Liev. He had the same tall, lean build, the same jet-black hair as Lawrence. The same quirky smile. But the whole package was fresher, softer, like a younger brother. Not so jaded, or cynical. Still, she had to know. She asked him point-blank. "So did you come from my century as well?"

Liev shook his head in a slow movement that made his slightly long hair curl on his shirt collar. If they were two hundred years in the future, the men still wore shirts and pants. Although outside of the fact that material covered both his legs and chest, the clothing was unlike any she'd seen before. His weird-looking friend with the green mohawk could have been from any number of places in her time, so he looked odd but not that odd. Outside of the technology, like the elevator—and, God, how creepy had that been—the rooms she'd seen so far looked almost normal. High tech and definitely futuristic and with almost a movie scene look to the space with the massive wall of monitors and a wall length console instead of keyboards and individual desks. It's what had been outside that had shocked her. Flying cars? Rooftop rail systems from building to building while something else snaked around the building going up? And the weird bright reflective silverishness to the buildings? Maybe the city was even domed. She didn't look out the windows around her. In fact, she deliberately avoided looking around. Her gaze locked on Liev.

"I'm sorry. I don't know you." He tried for a friendly smile and added, "Yet."

She rolled her eyes. "You would say that."

He gave her a hand to help move her away from the mess. "You must be mistaking me for someone from your time."

"Yeah, right. Like you aren't the spitting image of Lawrence Blackburn."

Liev stiffened. "That *is* my last name. And Lawrence was a blackhearted ancestor of ours. I'm sorry if you were harmed by him. I can only assure you that I am not him in any way."

She stared at him. "Doesn't that figure? Well, at least tell me that he's dead. That would almost make this worth it."

"That I can do." He smiled and held out his hand as if to shake hers. "I'm Liev Blackburn, and Lawrence is definitely dust by now."

The younger guy bobbed his head up and down. The long skinny body bobbed in a matching tune. She wondered if he had an iPod or something in his ear because he seemed to move to some inner beat. He gave her a huge grin and said, "I'm Milo. Liev is my older brother."

Her gaze widened. "That is so wrong."

The smaller guy narrowed his gaze, confusion clouding his eyes. Liev said, "Wrong or not, it's true. Milo is also a genius."

She snorted at that. "Oh, right. That whole genius thing about creating some kind of time machine that snatched me out of my own life without my permission. Well, thanks for nothing. So, before we go too far down this road, how about you reverse the results and let me return to the time where I belong."

A long strange silence filled the room. She narrowed her gaze suspiciously. "Why did you say that's the beauty of this—that this isn't reversible?"

And Charming gave voice to her thoughts. Thankfully it came out in a garbled whisper. "Uh-oh."

Milo looked at his feet and shuffled from left to

right and back again. Yeah, he was guilty as hell. She switched to Liev. And he was staring at Milo.

"You didn't figure that you needed a way to reverse the process?" She motioned to the nonexistent elevator that had dumped her in this futuristic office around her and said in an ominous voice, "You figured anyone— any *female*—would be delighted to find herself yanked away from everyone and anything she holds dear into a foreign world where she has no way to support herself?" Her voice rose at the end to shrill tones. "Dependent on you two for my living?"

Both men winced in sync.

She lowered her voice and continued in an angry whisper, "And while I'm running up a list of questions, here is a biggie." She paused. "Why me?"

LIEV WAS NONPLUSSED. He didn't know what to do or say to this poor woman. Even shocked and over-whelmed, she was glaring at him and his brother, her back stiff, but holding it together. He admired that. She had grit. That was amazing given the era she was from. She knew his ancestor, a man who'd left a horrible legacy of infidelity and distrust. He had been a wily liar, cheat and eventually, he had sunk under multiple embezzlement charges before being stabbed later in life within the prison system. That she mistook him for that man was a huge insult. He tried to remind himself that he didn't know her and that she didn't know him, but she'd jumped to one hell of an assumption. And she was pissed. The tears, the loud voice, and the death grip she had on her pet also said she was terrified.

And that he could understand. His heart melted at her plight. This was not her fault. That was all on his brother, Milo.

It struck him then that ... she also looked familiar. Like very familiar. At least her facial features. That tiny delicate body and luminescent skin, no. But he hoped she'd become more familiar to him. Then it hit him. He reared back to study her closer. Was she the girl in his favorite photo? There were differences, but she was close, ... oh, so close. He wanted to pull it out of his pocket and compare it to her but didn't dare. He turned to glare at his brother, wanting to question him on the spot. But it wasn't the time. Still, it left him wondering, ... was it her?

She looked ready to cry, and a woman's tears broke him every time. He leaned forward and softened his voice. "Please. Let's go to our place. We can explain the facts and come up with a plan of how to fix it."

His words appeared to drain all the stuffing and the ire from her body. She curled in on herself hugging her pet tightly as she buried her face in the animal's fur. He reached out gently and touched her shoulder then nudged her forward. "It will be okay. Come with us and we'll sort this out."

She moved as he directed. Silent but passive. That

state worried him more than any he'd seen of her so far. Home was right around the corner. Thankfully it was in the same block as his office, with aboveground and underground access between the two. He liked to live close to his place of business.

He walked her forward a few more steps. "That's good. Just a little way to go. Please. Let me just get you in a place where we can talk privately."

At his wording, her compliance stalled and so did her footsteps.

He wanted to pick her up and carry her, but that damn pet of hers glared at him. He'd claw Liev's eyes out if he gave him a chance. With another firm nudge, he added, "Come on. You're safe with me."

And then they were there.

Milo entered first; then the young lady followed. Liev brought up the rear and reengaged the alarms, locking them in.

"Privacy on."

The buzzes and clicks told him that the security system had scanned the space and found it clean.

Feeling a tad better, he strode forward and poured himself a large shot of whiskey. And downed it.

He spun to glare at his brother. "Jesus, Milo. What will we do now?"

Milo collapsed onto the couch. The air couch lifted and fell as he settled into his preferred space somewhere in-between fully inflated and fully deflated then rose to float somewhere between floor and ceiling.

The young woman stood immobile in the center of the room. Ash-blond hair, fine-boned, but she moved well. Maybe she was a dancer? There'd been ire in her voice, and fire had spit from her eyes. So a lively and brave spirit was in there. In spite of the circumstances, Liev admitted he was intrigued.

"Welcome to our home," he said gently. "Now, I introduced the two of us, Milo and I'm Liev. Please, won't you tell us—what's your name?"

She spun slowly. "Lani Summerland, of course."

Silence.

It took her a moment, then she got it. "You brought me into your world, and you don't even know who I am?" The shocked horror in her voice hit him hard. Then he saw the hurt in her eyes. Contrarily he wanted to enfold her in his arms and hold her close. To tell her that it was all okay. To let her know he wouldn't desert her. That it would work out fine.

But he'd never been a liar before, and he wasn't about to start now.

"I didn't choose you. Milo did." He motioned to his wacky brother, floating suspended in the middle of the room, his mohawk hanging over the edge of the now-deep-purple airbed. His eyes were closed, as if he'd dropped off to sleep.

"Milo did? And what the hell is he laying on? Whatever it is, I want one too." Her body swayed in protest to being vertical. "It wasn't purple, and it wasn't floating when we walked in."

"No, it wasn't." Liev sighed. Life had changed a lot since her era. "That's only one of the many things you'll have to get used to now."

She shook her head and said in a forlorn voice, "That's just it. I don't think I can."

CHAPTER 5

"N EVER MIND. LET'S just shelve this for the moment." Lani tried to straighten up, but her legs had taken on a rubbery sensation and refused to hold her properly. She clutched Charming even tighter. That he didn't complain worried her, but she was too overwhelmed to process what to do to help him. "I don't know if this is a delayed reaction, different oxygen in the air, or ..." Then her brain shut down. "I don't know," she whispered. "I don't feel so good."

The room swayed and circled around her.

"Easy." Liev grabbed her and led her toward the side of the room. Charming sagged against her, his weight increasing by the second. "You can stay in here. You need to rest. I don't think traveling through time was easy on your system."

"You think?" She laughed brokenly, but even her voice sounded odd. "Did your genius brother consider the damage to my DNA? That the reconstituted cells of my body didn't pull together the same way that it was when taken apart?"

"Nothing like that was supposed to happen." He motioned to the doorway in front of them. At least that's what the rectangle looked like. "The bedroom is through there. And chances are your body is fine. It just needs time to adjust."

She didn't have the energy to argue. And, with every step, her body got heavier. The effort to lift one foot after another was almost beyond her. Before she understood what was happening, Liev was helping her to a long white surface. She desperately wanted a bed to sleep in, but being horizontal on any surface would do. The sleep would follow regardless. She shifted the limp Charming in her arms, struggling to hold him now. Her arms were rubbery and her fingers were losing their grip.

"I think I need a doctor," she whispered. "I think there is something seriously wrong with me."

"We don't have doctors anymore," Liev said. "At least not like you mean. Our health care is very different today."

"Great. In the future, there are no doctors. Now really make my day and tell me there are no lawyers either." After all, Lawrence had been a lawyer.

Suddenly they'd reached the white object, and damn if he didn't push her on top of it.

"A hero you're not."

She felt more than saw his surprised look; then her own shock took over as the white surface softened and stretched, supporting the contours of her body like she'd never felt before. "What is this thing?" she whispered.

"A bed."

How that could be, she didn't know, and she no longer cared as the bed cradled her aching body just in time. Charming crashed spread-eagle on her chest, her arms fell to the side and with a soft groan, her eyes drifted closed, and she let go.

Into a deep sleep.

LIEV STARED DOWN at the impossible woman, proof of this impossible situation, brought on by his impossible little brother. Lani didn't look well. Her skin had a gray pasty look to it, and there were large dark circles under her eyes. There was a frailness to her he hadn't noticed initially. And that animal in her arms ... it collapsed sprawled out on her chest ... dead. He reached over hesitantly to check if it was still alive. Just as his fingers went to brush the thick fur, the animal shifted stretching out a paw as far as it would go as a tummy deep sigh escaped.

He didn't have an exclusive medical unit here. If he had, she'd be lying in it right now. There was one in the building. His friend Johan Strand owned it. If he was away, Liev would have taken her there instead of here. But Johan was home, and he'd be entertaining—like he always did.

Walking to the door, he cast a last look at the sleeping beauty. Compared to today's enhanced and cosmetically perfect women, she had character. She wasn't stunning. But she was pretty. Huge eyes that showed every emotion, a nose that turned up at the end ever-so-slightly, and a mobile mouth that caught his attention and held it whenever he was with her.

What would he do with her? Liev left her to talk to his brother. "Damn it, Milo. What are we going to do?"

No answer. He walked over to find his brother either deep in contemplation or … asleep.

"Milo?"

No answer. He walked closer to find that his brother had his headset strapped on to his virtual-reality goggles. Damn. He was in the zone. Now was it the game zone or the creative zone? Except, with Milo, there was often no difference. Only this was no time to duck out. He reached across his brother's body and pulled off the goggles.

"Hey." Milo tried to snag them from Liev.

But Liev held them out of reach. On a hunch, he put them against his eyes and gazed through them. Two young, lithe females cavorted in front of him with come-on gestures, enticing him to join them.

"Hell, Milo." He tossed the VR set on his brother's chest. "This is hardly the time for a sex romp."

"Hey. It's always time, bro." Milo went to put them back on his face when Liev grabbed them again and tossed them across the room.

Milo roared.

"Damn. Get serious." Liev planted his hands on his

hips and glared at his outraged brother. "We have a problem here. A big one. You know she's sick, right? Like seriously sick. Like she could be dead by morning?"

"Nah. She's fine." Milo stood and stretched and sidled to where his goggles were. "I'll head to bed now."

"Touch those goggles and I'll lose them permanently the next time you are out of the room."

Milo froze. "Hey, that's not fair. I do some of my best thinking when I'm sex … in a playful mood."

With a snort, Liev shook his head. "Like hell. You say you do your best thinking as an excuse to do whatever the hell you want." He reached his brother in seconds, grabbed him by the shoulder, and gave him a shake. "Stop kidding around. We have to solve this problem."

Milo cringed and stepped back, out of his brother's reach. "We don't have a problem. I brought her here for you. Therefore, you have a problem." With that, Milo snagged his goggles and walked from the room.

For him? Liev stared after his brother in shock. And once again brought up the question of Lani's identity in relationship to the photo.

But his brother was gone. Walking away from something he didn't like. Didn't want to deal with. Dumping the problem on someone else's shoulders. Again. In this case—Liev's shoulders. Again.

Being sixteen forever was getting old. At least for those who had to live with Milo.

Liev tilted his head back and closed his eyes, waiting for the anger to drain and some reasonable next step to rise up from the depths of his own impressive brain.

Bottom line, she was hurting. And he was indirectly responsible. How could he help her? There really was only one way. She needed a medical pod. And fast.

That meant Johan. His longtime friend walked a fine line between legal and illegal business activities. So far he was doing well with it. They both had a hatred for the Council and the multitude of government regulations being stuffed down their throats.

He glanced at the time. Maybe, just maybe, Johan hadn't started partying yet.

It was worth a try. In person or by comp? Comp would be faster.

He punched in Johan's name. And closed his eyes briefly when Johan's face filled the screen. "Hey. Glad I caught you."

"What's up, Liev?" Johan's bright, inquisitive grin popped out. "Looking to hook up tonight? I've got some prime flesh coming by soon."

"No. No. I've got some of my own here, but she's sick. I was hoping to use your unit." He waited a moment and then, in a quiet voice, added, "Please."

"Sure. No problem." Johan nodded agreeably. "You know the code. Go for it. With any luck, I won't need it tonight."

Liev wiped a shaky hand across his forehead. "Thanks, Johan. I won't forget this."

"No biggie. If she doesn't pick up, and you're still looking for some action, there will be plenty here all night long."

"As usual." In an effort to appease his friend, he added, "We'll see. I might pop by later on."

"Pod is empty now, so go for it." Johan's face blinked out.

As he closed his comm, Liev wondered about the sensibility of waiting until later. But how would he get her up there when she was out cold? Liev returned to where Lani slept. He frowned at the critter guarding her. How could he get her to the healing pod without that?

Then the critter dropped its head on Lani's chest, like the weight of his head was too heavy to hold. And Liev realized that the critter had endured just as harsh a trip as Lani. It probably needed the healing pod too.

That could really be tricky. He could use the elevator to get them all up there, and the healing pod had a room all to itself, but would the critter cooperate? Would Lani stay asleep for this?

It would be best if she did.

He really was out of options. And out of time. He opened a cupboard and pulled out a blanket. With some difficulty, he managed to wrap up the two newcomers. He lifted them both into his arms, more disturbed than he realized when neither moved. Maybe they were badly injured internally. His gut twisted. He should've done this earlier.

He raced outside his apartment. "Stealth mode on." The elevator swooped down, encompassing them all. "Johan's healing pod."

The cube took off silently.

They'd made it this far. He hoped the rest would be so easy. The elevator delivered him outside Johan's pod room. He stepped in, relieved to find the room empty and the pod open. He laid his lightweight burden down gently, realizing as he did so how delicate her frame was. Even the critter was deceptive looking, in that he appeared big and bulky. He carried so much fur on his body, and the face appeared to have been flattened in the birthing process, but, as far as actual poundage went, her pet weighed almost nothing.

And maybe muscle and bone-density loss was a side effect of the time-travel. He didn't know if the pod could heal that. It was a little out of the generic pod's scope.

He walked over to the door, closing and locking it behind him. Then he turned his attention to the two comatose patients on the table. He closed the lid of the pod on them, blanket and all, and walked to the diagnostic table. "Start scanning," he instructed the computer.

The machine made a weird beeping sound, then said, "The blanket and outer clothing of the patients must be removed."

"Scan patients in the condition they are in," he said.

"We cannot," chimed the robotic voice. "Something is stopping the scan from initializing. Please remove the blankets and outer clothing."

"Damn." He returned to the pod, opened the lid, and, with difficulty, he tugged the blanket free. Lani wore pants of some stretchy material and a short-sleeve shirt. He didn't want to remove it if he didn't have to. "Start scan."

The beeps picked up, and a blue laser light started at Lani's head and swept down to her feet. Liev breathed a sigh of relief. Good, it worked with her dressed. "Scan results?"

"Patients are experiencing an extreme reaction to the atmosphere. Muscle weakness, rapid heart rate, and irregular breathing indicate a reaction to high stress."

"Tell me something I don't know," he muttered. "Will she be all right?"

"Patient is exhausted. We are giving her high doses of vitamins and lowering her vital signs. Sleep is paramount. Her body has undergone a great shock. We are adding her condition to our database."

"No," he snapped. "Cancel that. Do not add her condition to the database."

"It is protocol," stated the computer. "This is a condition we have not encountered. It must be added."

"Shit. Shit. No!" he said urgently. "Do not add at this time. Should the patient not recover quickly, then it can be added. Everyone reacts to stress differently. This is hers."

"This is most unusual."

"Yeah, that's me." Liev walked over to Lani. "What about the critter? What is its condition?"

"He appears to be suffering the same muscle weakness as the woman. Also the same increased heart rate." The computer stopped, then added, "Interesting."

"Do not add this to the database," he snapped.

The robotic voice spoke again. "We must. It is protocol."

Frustration rolled through him. "And yet, like the woman, the critter will likely be fine."

"If that is true, why did you bring them here?"

And what was he doing, arguing with a healing pod? Computers had taken over his world. They now argued and chastised and nagged like an old fish wife.

"I wanted to make sure that there was no internal damage," he muttered.

"We did not scan for that."

He stopped and turned to look at the console. "Why not?"

"You did not remove her clothing. We could not go through all the material."

"That's crap. Of course you can."

"We do not know this particular blend of materials. We must add it to the database."

He was going to pull his hair out. "Do not add it to your database."

"We must. It is—"

"Protocol, yeah, I know." He walked over to the pod. "If you are done with the booster shot, I'll take off her shirt and pants. Then you can do a deeper scan."

"Acknowledged."

At least *that* wasn't breaking protocol. He opened the pod and tugged her boots off her feet. Then he opened the closures on her pants and tugged them off. He swallowed at the sight of the purple underclothes. Yeah, lingerie hadn't changed much in the last couple of centuries. It was as sexy back then as it is now. Walking to the side of the pod, he opened up the buttons that held Lani's shirt closed and spread apart the material. He could feel his own heart rate increase at the sight of her firm breasts rising from the matching purple bra. Crap, he felt like a pervert.

But she was something.

"Can you do a complete scan with her like this?" He rearranged the critter down the long, lean length of her, its head resting against her ribs. If she woke to find the critter dying or missing, then there would likely be hell to pay.

"We can."

"Good. Then please complete the full diagnostics."

He closed the pod lid, and the blue laser light swept slowly down the length of the bed. Then it reversed all the way back up.

"Scan complete," said the computer.

"And the scan results?" Liev asked.

"The patient has no severe internal damage. There have been some recent adaptations to her physical body that we have not seen before."

There was a hum. "We have added that information to our database."

"No," he shouted. "Damn it, do not add it the database."

"It is protocol."

He dropped his forehead against the glass top of the pod, wanting to smash his fist against the smooth unyielding surface. "And what of the critter?"

"The same odd changes have also recently been done to its body. We have added this information to the database."

He didn't bother arguing. He'd try to wipe the memory after he was done. "What kind of changes have been made?"

"We do not have a scan from before these changes in order to say." The robotic voice was not being helpful.

"Right. Then how do you know changes have been made?"

"There are signs of new tissue," continued the computer. "Signs of healed muscle and skin. The DNA has been altered."

He swallowed on that last bit. Milo had said that wouldn't happen. Then he'd probably worded it in such a way as to avoid an outright lie and still not tell the truth. "Are these changes dangerous?"

"Not that we can see at this time." A series of monotone clicks repeated, as if the console was shutting down.

"So is she healthy?" Liev asked urgently before it turned off. "Good to leave?"

The clicks paused. "She is exhausted. She must rest for twenty-four hours minimum." The robotic voice stopped, as if considering its next words. Then added, "Maybe longer."

He didn't want to consider how this console's actions imitated human thinking. "And can you help her do that?"

"It is done."

With a sigh of relief, Liev opened the pod, gathered up her clothing, and wrapped both Lani and the critter in the blanket, along with her clothes. And stepped out into the hallway.

Just as she woke up.

CHAPTER 6

THE BOUNCING AROUND woke her up. Lani forced her eyes open. Heavy and unwieldy, they didn't want to obey her orders. But it felt like she was being carried. Only to find she was tucked up against a man's chest, carried like she was a precious child.

She'd been sleeping so soundly; then the nightmares had kicked in, and she'd surfaced, feeling like she'd been through the worst night of her life.

As the memories drifted in, she wondered if she had.

Except for the male carrying her. *Liev*. His name drifted through her consciousness. He smelled so wonderful. And the strength, the ease with which he carried her, ... he wasn't even breathing hard.

His heartbeat pounded under her ear. Slow, steady, and strong.

She sighed happily. She didn't know who he was or where she was, but this part was good. Momentarily she could forgive his role in this nightmare. She sighed happily once again.

Until the pain penetrated her consciousness. Everything ached. Had this person hurt her? Was she in danger? It didn't feel like it. But then …

Her body was jostled again, … and that set parts of her to hurting in the worst way. Bones ached. Joints throbbed. Muscles burned. She tried to shift away from the pain. She moaned.

"Easy, Lani." Lowering his head slightly, Liev whispered, "Take it easy. We're almost back. Just lie still."

"Where?" she murmured. "Back where?"

"Back to bed. I took you to the healing pod. It should have helped."

"I hurt. Everywhere." She shifted her legs restlessly. She wanted it to stop. "Put me down." Then her voice broke at the pain. "Please."

"*Shh*. It's all right. You'll be fine. We're almost home."

Home sounded good. She felt the urgency in his movements as he walked faster. He was worried, racing somewhere. Then the air changed, calmed. Liev slowed down immediately.

In the background, she heard him call out, "Stealth on."

She was taken into a darker room. Her eyes were open only a slit, enough to see the atmosphere change but not enough to see the details of her surroundings. She opened her eyes wider, happy it appeared to be easier to do now. Her body was jostled again before being laid down on a hard surface. Immediately, she cried out as pain radiated into the corners of her body. "Oh, it's hard. It hurts."

The surface softened, cradled her, eased her pain. She sighed in relief, her body shuddering in reaction.

"It's okay now," he said. "You're back in bed. Just rest."

She tried to shift, her arms struggling with the blanket, until something big and furry was placed in her arms. She whispered happily, "Charming."

He made no reply, but she knew it was him, and his soft, gentle breathing reassured her that he was well. Now if only her body would stop screaming at her. She rolled over, felt something tugged up and placed atop her shoulders, and then soft, gentle music filled the room.

"Sleep. You'll feel better in the morning."

That made sense. She let herself drift away.

Until a few hours later, when she woke up in agony. Pain radiated throughout her body. She'd never done much jogging, but her body felt like she'd done a full marathon. And it complained bitterly. Barely cognizant that she was only in her underwear, she stumbled to a doorway that led to the bathroom, tears running down her cheeks. By the time she was back in bed, she could barely move. With every step, her muscles had seized up a little more. Charming lay in the bed motionless, his huge eyes wells of pain.

"I know how you feel, buddy." She stopped and considered what she just did. "I had to use the bathroom. What about you?"

He had to go sometime. If he hadn't already. She

didn't want to check the corners of the room too closely. "What can I do about a litter box for you, Charming?"

She looked around, but nothing resembling a decent container would work for this purpose. She thought about the bathroom. "Charming, can you use the toilet?"

He shuddered and gave her a horrified look. "Water is in the toilets."

She winced. Actually, she wasn't sure water was in this bowl. She'd noticed a blue jelly substance she'd refused to check out any closer. "I know. But we have no sand or litter here. I don't know what to do for you."

Charming stood and jumped off the bed. He landed, then collapsed. She cried out and reached over to pick him up. "Our muscles don't work right here."

"Yeah, I got that," he grumbled. "How about that litter box thing?"

"How about a water one?" she asked hopefully.

The horrified look in his eyes made her laugh.

"I have to go," he growled. "Let's take a look at it."

She carried him into the bathroom. It had taken her a bit of time to figure out the system. She had no idea how to help him understand. The seat seemed to adapt to the size of the butt sitting down. Kind of like the couch and the bed. She opened the lid so he could see the seat, then perched him on top.

"This is what there is. You go pee in the hole."

He stared at her.

She gave him a winning smile, and said, with bright encouragement, "You can do this."

"So not."

"I'll just leave you so you can have some privacy."

And she escaped.

Oh, Lord. What was she doing here? They both wanted to go home. They didn't belong here. They couldn't even move properly. How the heck were they supposed to survive? They had no papers, no identification, no family or friends. No job and—worse yet—no money. If such a thing still existed. And then there were those two idiots who'd brought her and Charming here. They weren't to be trusted.

On the heels of that thought, she sat on the bed and remembered the strength of those arms, the soothing tone in Liev's voice as he had told her to rest. He'd been gentle. Caring. That was very sexy. A man who looked after you when you were hurt and hurting was something special.

If only he hadn't been part of the plot to bring her here.

He said he'd had nothing to do with it, but ...

And, speaking of which, she planned to nail Milo tomorrow and find out how and why she'd been chosen.

She had no great skills. She was no beauty. She had left no legacy—at least at the time of her kidnapping. And that was on top of the dismal overview of her life to date that Milo had read off earlier. How had they even known who she was to swoop down and scoop her up?

A weird scratching sound came from the direction of the bathroom, followed by a heavy *thud*, which hinted that Charming was done with his business. As he strolled out, heavy limbed, his head dipped lower with every step. She winced and then headed toward him. Slowly. "See? It wasn't so bad."

"It so was," he said darkly. "What kind of place is this that they don't have a decent dry litter box?" He walked toward her and twined around her legs. "Do you realize how long it's been since we ate?" He plunked his furry butt down on the weird tiled floor and stared up at her. "Do you think they know what food is? If they haven't heard about litter boxes ..."

How typical. His stomach was always a priority. "I'm sure they know what food is. Chances are good we might even recognize some of it."

He shot her a horrified look, jumped up on the bed, and proceeded to turn around in circles before collapsing. "I'm going back to sleep. Maybe when I wake up the next time, this nightmare will be over."

"That's a good idea."

All she could hear was his heavy breathing. She climbed up beside him and curled herself around his pudgy body. She really wanted her life back. To be back in her tiny apartment, getting ready for her date. She'd been so excited ...

How could they take that away from her?

And she fell asleep once more.

LIEV GROANED AND rolled over yet again. His mind wouldn't shut off. Although he had done his best to wipe Johan's pod of any evidence of his and Lani's earlier visit, Liev still wondered if the pod's treatment would work. He had no idea how to stop this mess from changing his life as he knew it. His brother had done the unthinkable. At the same time, it was a major scientific achievement—and no one could ever know.

His brilliance had to stay hidden. It was too dangerous to let the world know.

And what was he supposed to do with Lani? This charming young woman hadn't asked for her life to be destroyed at Milo's whim. Liev didn't even know how she'd been chosen. She wasn't Milo's usual choice when it came to women. Lani had no visible piercings, and her hair was all the same color.

Then again, Milo had mentioned that he'd picked Lani for Liev. That brought the old photo to mind again. Was he so pathetic that his kid brother felt he needed to get Liev a girlfriend? Sure, Liev was going through a dry spell, but that was by choice. He didn't like Johan's party scene. It had been fun once or twice, but he preferred to be with a woman because he liked her, not because she had the requisite body parts.

And—he twisted his lips in a dour smile—he was a romantic. Old-fashioned. He wanted to love and to be loved. Was that so impossible?

He rolled over again. How could he stop the world from finding out about Milo's accomplishment? He also had to stop Milo from repeating his actions. But he needed to find a way to send Lani home first. Although Liev wouldn't mind if she stayed for a bit—if she wanted to.

Was it wrong of him to want her to stay? Instantly he crushed that thought. She wasn't meant to stay here. He didn't dare get attached to her. She wasn't a pet. He couldn't just keep her.

But a part of him was considering it.

Just as the morning light drifted into his room, and he thought he might finally go to sleep, a pounding came at his front door. Groaning, he pulled on a shirt and pants. When the noise came a second time, he stumbled to the door, calling out, "Hang on. I'm coming."

He pulled open the door, his hand hiding a yawn. And froze.

Two suits with cold flat stares stood there with a crumpled looking Johan sandwiched between them. Liev glanced at Johan, a question in his eyes, but asked the two others in a genial voice, "What's up, gentlemen?"

One man said, "You're wanted for questioning at the Council." His tone was stiff, uncompromising. Just like the look on the first man's face. Liev glanced at the second man's stony expression. Council henchmen. Great. He was in trouble again. He cast his mind back to see where he had messed up. And how to recover ...

Liev frowned at his friend. "Johan, what's going on?"

Johan shrugged but wore his customary careless grin. "Damned if I know. I was trying to sleep off my party when they came knocking. I'm being hauled in too."

Not good. Liev straightened, looked at the first man, and said, "Do I need my lawyers, gentlemen?"

"If you feel you need one, you may certainly call in representation, as is your right. However, at this moment, while we are requesting your presence at the Council, it is not an order."

The unspoken "yet" hung in the air.

"Right. Give me a moment. I'll get dressed and meet you there."

The second suit, who'd yet to speak, said, "No. We will wait and escort you there."

So this was serious. Liev nodded and returned to his bedroom. He swallowed a booster, hoping to make up for his lousy night. He walked to his wardrobe, where he pulled out a suit and dressed carefully. Milo did creative. Liev did power and intimidation.

After a quick glance around, he pocketed his comp and walked out. He needed Lani and her critter to stay asleep for this. Hopefully he wouldn't be too long. He could count on Milo not surfacing for a few hours yet.

Johan at his side, the four men traveled to the Council building and were escorted into the inner office immediately.

No waiting. No coffee offered. Immediate reception.

This was very serious.

They were led forward to face four Councilmen, all seated on a raised podium, watching as Liev's group approached.

Liev recognized all four of them. His stomach sank. He didn't exactly have a good relationship with the Council after Milo broke protocol over a year ago. Except for one member, Stephen Cavendish, a junior member who was also an old friend. As a junior member, his presence on the Council was sporadic.

No sound was heard for a long moment as the Councilmen assessed him and Johan. One of the two Councilmen in the middle finally spoke up. "Johan and Liev, thank you both for coming. We understand that a disturbance occurred on the health pod registered to you, Johan."

Ah, shit.

So much for his orders to that damn computer. It hadn't wiped the data and had instead submitted it as per protocol, and his attempts to fix it afterward hadn't effectively amended those either. That had raised flags. He'd expected the power outage to have done that. Although there'd been several of those lately, unrelated to Milo's work. He frowned. Or were they? Had Milo tested his program out earlier?

Johan raised his hands, palms outward. "Anything is possible. It experienced heavy use last night as several of my guests took advantage of my personal unit. In fact, likely a dozen or so could have used my pod. I had a big party, and many people, not having their own pod, come specifically for that purpose. I don't mind. I never have."

"You will have no problem supplying us a list of your guests then?" the speaker asked, who Liev thought was called Carlson, peering over his glasses at Johan.

Liev wondered at the glasses. No one used them for vision anymore. Chances were good the speaker was running all kinds of scans on Johan right now. From financials to health statistics. The speaker settled back with a frown, removing the glasses.

That was interesting. Liev turned slightly to study the man at his side. Did Johan have a way to block the scan? If so …

"I'll get as many names as I can, but I have an open-door policy with regard to guests." Johan gave them a fat grin. "The more, the merrier." He held his hands up in appeal. "What is this about?"

"Data from the pod proposed a few questions last night. We are obligated to check it out further." Again the man lifted his glasses to study the two men. And again frowned and took them off to lay on the desk in front of him.

Johan's eyebrows shot up. "Interesting." He glanced over at Liev and shrugged.

"And I'm here why?" Liev asked coolly.

"We have information that you asked to use the pod last night."

Not good. Liev tilted his head slightly. "That is correct. And what regulation did you violate to find that information?"

Johan snorted. "That's a damn good question. Are you recording my calls?" he asked in outrage. He pulled out his comp and jotted down notes. "That is something I will be looking into."

"In the case of issues of national security, we are within our rights to record calls."

"National security?" Liev spluttered. Inside, his nerves jangled. "What are you talking about?" He pulled out his comp and sent a nudge to his own lawyer, Hahn Driscoll. With any luck, he could keep this tied up long enough to solve the problem. Liev also checked to make sure his comp was recording this session. That was just a basic precaution he'd used since the last blow up.

"We don't have enough information to complete a full analysis of the problem. The data stream from the pod was corrupted. We must also investigate a massive power outage that occurred earlier on that same date."

"Ha, corrupt data is the norm half the time. And lately there have been more power outages than not. You know that." Johan laughed. "Any one of my many guests could have broken it." He shook his head. "You will also note that I have it repaired on a regular basis."

"We will follow up on the guest list you supply. If you have no further information to offer, you are dismissed."

And that tone of voice had Liev's back going up. He glared at the four men staring down at him, identical looks on their faces. But this was not the time or place to start an all-out war. He'd warred with these men before. Milo often got into trouble.

And Liev always worked to get him out of it.

He wasn't sure that was possible this time.

Johan tugged his arm. "Come on, buddy. It's time to get a coffee. Let these guys worry about national security." He snickered. "Coffee is on me."

Liev let his friend tug him outside. Besides, it would give Liev a chance to ask Johan if he could block scans and if he would share that technology with Liev. They went through the austere building in complete silence, but, once outside, Johan lost it. "They were monitoring our freaking phone calls? They will not get away with that."

"Sorry if I got you into this."

"Ha, it probably wasn't even you. Dozens of people were in that thing last night." Johan shook his head. "Besides, I'm glad you did. I need those bloodsucking lawyers to earn their retainers. I've been paying them for years, and they do nothing. This"—he held up his comp—"is not allowed."

He glared at Liev. "Do you know how many laws they've broken? Do you have any idea how many secrets of mine they might have uncovered?"

Liev was surprised at the sheer level of fury in his friend's voice. Maybe he had a reason. Maybe he was hiding something. Liev didn't care. He was hiding something himself.

A light rain drizzled on the two men. Liev looked up, surprised to see a storm gathering above the buildings. Flash storms were unusual here when the weather was computer controlled.

Johan motioned to the sky. "It's been going on since late yesterday." His face twisted as he studied it. "Wonder what the hell is going on."

Liev's stomach knotted. *Please let it have nothing to do with Milo's damn experiment. Please.* "No idea," he said lightly.

Johan motioned across the street where the coffee shop was. "I know I mentioned coffee, but, if you don't mind, I'll take a rain check."

I'll ask him about blocking scans later. "Not a problem. I've got to get to work as it is."

Johan slapped him on the shoulder. "It's been a weird morning already. Let's hope it improves." And he walked away. His long legs ate up the distance. Johan had a specific goal, and his temper still rode his emotions.

Liev hoped Johan and his lawyer would raise a little hell. Liev planned to do just that himself.

After he checked up on Milo and Lani.

CHAPTER 7

L ANI WOKE UP slowly, her eyes drifting open, then sliding closed again. Only to come awake to wild green hair framing a looming face. She screamed and bolted upward. Trapped by the wrappings, she fell sideways onto the soft mattress. Expecting to fall and still trying to get away, she crab-walked backward to escape on a bed that seemed to grow in the direction she moved. Criminy.

"Calm down. I was just looking to see if you were awake." Milo danced back as Lani retreated a little more. "Hey, I'm not here to hurt you."

Lani took a deep breath and tried to shake off the panic of waking up to a strange face looming over her. "Why couldn't you just call out to me?"

"I did." He held his hands up in front of him. "Sorry. I should have called out louder."

She shuddered and slowly sat up. "Yeah, okay. I'm awake." She pushed her long hair out of her eyes. "Now why did you wake me up?"

"I didn't want to." He stepped back again. "I was just taking a look."

She stared. "At me? While I was sleeping?" She

glanced down and gasped. She only had on her under-clothes. And the fallen blanket had left much of her exposed. She snatched the cover and clutched it to her chest before glaring at Milo.

"No. No. I wasn't looking. Honest." He shook his head, a blush climbing up his neck and face. "Liev called. He wanted to know if you were up. So I came to look. That's it."

"Well, I am now." She stared at the weird bed. And caught sight of Charming curled into a still fur ball. "Charming," she cried out and scrambled over to him. Gently she stroked his still form and almost bawled when she realized that he was breathing. "I was so scared that you'd died during the night," she said to him.

"He shouldn't die." Milo interrupted their cuddle to add, "His DNA may have changed a bit, but he will live a long life."

Lani shot him a disgusted look. "You have no idea how he's changed."

"And he won't ever know if you don't tell him," Charming muttered in a strangled yowl. He opened his eyes and glared at her. "I could use some more sleep." He stretched out his front leg and yawned, then tucked up into a tight ball and went back to sleep.

Still smiling, she turned to stare up at Milo. Only his gaze whipped from the cat to her and back to the cat. Oh, shit. He'd heard.

"You can hear the cat talk," he whispered in awe.

"And, like, wow. It talks back."

"Right. Charming is special." That he'd heard Charming speaking wasn't perfect timing, but it's not like there would ever be a good time to bring up this. And Milo would have found out sometime. She snorted and shoved the bedding back to free her legs. "Now, if you don't mind, I have to go to the bathroom."

Flushing wildly, Milo backed up. "Sure. No problem." He gave one last fascinated stare at Charming and bolted toward the door. At the doorway, he paused. "Do you need anything?"

"You mean, like all my clothes from home? The shampoo and soap I love so I could enjoy a shower? Oh, and how about some food for me and Charming? And if you guys know what coffee is …"

Milo's eyes lit up. "I can do the coffee part. We have awesome coffee here."

"Well, that's good. At least you have something decent," she muttered as she pulled herself to the edge of the bed.

With that, Milo escaped for the kitchen. She hoped.

Her legs were slow and shaky, but at least they held when she stood up. Only the bathroom looked damn far away.

When she was done, she all but collapsed on the bed. She couldn't help but be grateful a toilet was still a toilet. Then they hadn't changed much from the centuries before her time either.

She'd barely covered up again, the bed softening

and curling around her, when Milo returned, carrying a tray with both hands. She eyed him suspiciously. Was he trying to make her feel better, or was this normal behavior in his time? If so, then obviously she knew of a few good things about living here. Still, she figured he was working on that whole *keep her happy theme* so she didn't explode on him. She could work with that.

"Here is coffee and a snack. Liev is on his way home. We'll eat then."

She stared at the pretty setting and the tiny cup on her tray. If she didn't know better, she'd have thought she was in Europe, having a cup of espresso. She picked it up and took an experimental sniff. It smelled like coffee.

"It's safe," Milo said. He bounced from side to side. "Go ahead. Try it."

She eyed him over the rim of her tiny cup. Why was he so excited? She studied the rich liquid suspiciously. Then took a tiny sip. And sighed. Oh, joy. They actually had real coffee. She almost melted with her second sip, and, by the time she'd reached the bottom of the minuscule cup, she was looking for more.

Milo disappeared and returned immediately with a small silver pot. He refilled her cup and took a step back. She glared at him. Then at the pot. Still in his grip. And back at him.

He swallowed. "Sure. I'll just leave the pot here. You can have as much as you want." He gingerly added it to her tray.

"Thank you, that's very generous of you," she murmured, keeping a close eye on him. "And you're right. It is good coffee."

He beamed. "Thank you."

"Did you make it?"

Confusion made his smile go away. "Umm, I guess."

Okay, smaller steps. "Did you grind the beans and pour water into a pot, measure the coffee, and start it dripping?" At least that's how coffee used to be made at her apartment and at most of her jobs.

He shook his head so fast the bright green Mohawk waved in the wind like a hand. "No. No. I just pushed a button."

Interesting. Then again she should expect that everything here would be computerized, technological advancement being what it was. She should probably be grateful she hadn't been dragged into the Flintstones' era.

Coffee like this with a push of a button definitely had something going for it.

"Hello? Lani?" Liev called out. "Are you here?"

Really? Where else would she be? That was one huge world out there, and she had no money and no ID. It would take a braver person than her to venture out there alone.

Milo bubbled out with, "We're in her bedroom."

Yeah, like she always entertained men in her bedroom.

Just then Charming sat up and stretched out a paw. She watched as he hooked the treat Milo had added to her tray. It appeared to be a sweet bun of some kind, but she'd yet to try it. She wasn't sure her stomach could handle anything solid right now. But she wanted to. Her last meal had been a long time ago.

Liev filled the doorway.

"Isn't this awfully cozy looking," he said coolly, his deep purple eyes taking in everything, assessing it all.

She lifted her chin. "Milo offered me coffee, and I took him up on it."

"Liev, what happened this morning?" Milo asked worriedly. "I heard the door, and, just like that, you were gone."

Lani studied Liev's face. He looked everywhere but at her.

"It was about me—wasn't it?" And she knew. Somehow, someone had found out. "What did you tell them?"

He looked straight at her, then walked forward several steps. "Nothing."

Milo stepped between the two of them. His gaze darted from one to the other. He asked his brother, "What did you say?"

"Nothing." He ran his hand through his dark curls. "They asked a few questions, and I answered. They didn't ask about you specifically, so I didn't have to lie."

Milo bounced forward. "What did they ask about?"

Looking very uncomfortable, Liev said, "They asked

about the pod."

"What pod?" Milo stepped forward to look into his brother's face. "Liev, what pod?"

"Johan's healing pod. I took Lani up there last night. She was hurting. I figured, if she had sustained internal damage due to the time-travel, the pod could heal her."

"Oh, no. Oh, no." Milo danced backward in horror. "No, you didn't. Please say you didn't."

"Considering you refuse to have a pod of our own, I didn't have much choice. Also, considering you dragged her through a wormhole and dumped her here, her body is suffering. Did you even consider the impact on her physical body?"

Lani watched the brothers. Liev, the older and more responsible. Milo, the younger incorrigible genius with little sense of reality. He'd been protected so much that he wasn't held accountable for all his actions. Like what he'd done to her.

And Liev was doing his best. She spoke up. "I'm sorry for your troubles, taking me to this pod, but thank you for thinking of me and my health."

Both brothers turned to stare at her. She gave a little finger wave. "Yeah, I'm here too. Remember?"

"So, if we'd had a pod," Milo said slowly, "this wouldn't ever have happened?"

Liev snorted. "No. *And*, if you'd listened to me in the first place, *this* wouldn't have happened."

Milo's face twisted in thought. Moodily Liev kicked

the door. "Besides, a pod is being delivered today."

"No, no. I hate them." Milo backed up, shaking his hands wildly in front of him. "They are dangerous. We can't have one."

"Well, too bad," Liev snapped. "You should have thought of that before you hurt Lani."

Milo spun around to look at Lani. "I didn't hurt her."

"Yes, you did. And she's still suffering. For all we know, she could have long-term health issues. She needs our help now."

"But a pod will be connected to *them* ..." Milo hissed.

"No." Liev smiled. "This one is unregistered."

Milo gasped, hot color flooding his face. "But that's ... illegal!"

It was Liev's turn to stare at his brother. "A little too late to worry about that now," he said.

Lani laughed at Liev's glare. "You two are obviously brothers."

Both turned to glare at her.

She shrugged and took another sip of coffee. "So, when is this healing pod arriving? Because you're right. I could sure use it. Not to mention some food."

"You just had a snack and coffee," Milo protested.

"How about real food now?" Lani stared at the crumbs Charming had left her and sighed. "Like eggs, bacon, some hash browns?" At Milo's disgusted look, she smiled hopefully and added, "Even toast sounds wonderful."

"We don't eat garbage like that anymore. We care about our bodies here. We drink synthetic and highly nutritious shakes now."

"Only shakes?" she asked in horror. "What about real food? Like fruit, veggies, fried chicken, cheesecake, ... and other essential foods."

Milo shuddered in revulsion. "I'm a vegetarian. As we all should be."

"See? That just won't work for me." She sat up in bed. Charming rolled over and stretched his paws. "I like food," Lani said. "Real food."

"And we have food," Liev said. "Real food. My brother has been this way since infancy. I, however, still eat real food."

She brightened. "Awesome. Any chance of some?" Her stomach took that moment to grumble and growl very loudly. She smiled hopefully. "And soon?"

Liev stared at her. His eyebrows shot up, and a big smile overtook his face. He said, "I can do that. I'll be a few minutes." He turned and left. The room seemed lonely, empty.

"Oh, that's great." Milo grinned. "He loves cooking. Now he has you to look after food-wise too."

Lani stared at him, then broke out laughing. "You mean, you guys are so advanced but you still have to cook?" For some reason, that struck her as funny. She laughed and laughed. "If I were home, I'd have picked up the phone and just ordered in."

"We have takeout too." Milo bounded closer. "High-end food."

"Yeah, sure," she scoffed, smoothing the pleats in her incredibly soft bedding. Now that she was awake she was taking note of the differences around her. Like the custom fitting bed, the butter soft bedding. The light colored walls that had a luminous glow. Was that the paint or the sunrise behind it? Not wanting to think about what was outside, she added, "Like the rest of your supposed advanced lifestyle."

"We do! Healing pods. Awesome elevators." He motioned to the tray with the coffee. "The best coffee ever. A technologically advanced society you couldn't even imagine. Climate controlled green lifestyle that was way past what you could have envisioned back in your time. And that's just for starters."

"I'll give you that on the coffee, but your lifestyle seriously sucks. Look at this tiny-ass apartment, the monster cities ..."

"Ha! Look what I did with you." Milo did a fast two-step. "See? Gotcha there."

Immediately the air cooled, and her smile fell away. She dropped her gaze. "Yeah, that's a big gotcha."

"*Uhmmm*, yeah. I'll go make more coffee." He scooted backward from the bedroom. Escaping ...

She let him go.

If Lani could get up and walk into the kitchen, she would help cook, but any movement seemed to steal all her energy. She sank back against the pillows. She felt like a fat slug whose body had grown so big, so heavy, it couldn't carry its own weight. Considering the look on her baby's face, she had to wonder if Charming didn't feel the same. She bent to scratch the back of his head. He rolled over slightly and stared at her, but the look in his eyes made her shift and tug him, blankets and all, into her arms.

His head fell back.

"Don't feel so good, do you? Do we?" she corrected. She nuzzled his neck, reassured when his engine kicked in and his heavy purr filled the room. "At least that much of you is working."

"Yes, but I'm tired." He closed his eyes and laid his head back down.

"Me too." She wondered what the pod had done for her last night when she still felt so rough today. Then again, maybe she wouldn't have woken up today without it. Apparently they had an unregistered pod being delivered today. What kind of a government system had pods register the medical knowledge and defects of its contents without the people knowing? There was such a thing as too much government intervention.

And would having an unregistered unit get the brothers into more trouble?

Then again, if they were found with a nonregistered person, ... she couldn't imagine having to explain her presence. Hell, she had no answers. She'd have to tell the truth about what she did know. And would likely end up in a psych ward.

Who'd believe her?

Who could?

At least the brothers could have brought her clothes with her. Then again, as she stared down at Charming, they had brought the most important part of her life. Presumably because she'd been holding on to him at the time. And, as she thought about it, when she was whooshed away from her apartment, she'd been wishing he could talk. Coincidence?

What had happened to her old life? Had anyone reported her missing? Did she just disappear forever? Was she a missing person in the history books? Or did the apartment blow up, and Milo's little time-travel trick caused the deaths of a couple hundred people? Could she find out? Would she do a search on the internet and find herself? Did they even have internet here?

And, if they did, would her search be reported to someone that she was researching this person in history? Did the government keep that close an eye on its citizens?

If they kept that close an eye on everyone's health—maybe.

She had a lot of questions and no answers. The biggest one was still unanswered—was this really a one-way trip?

LIEV WORKED IN the kitchen, quietly and competently at the counter. She needed food. It would be these mundane details that would keep him focused. Maybe while doing the mundane, he'd come up with a solution for everything else. He glanced up at the screen on the wall. Still a half hour until the pod was delivered.

He didn't want anyone else to see it. He'd asked for a call when the delivery left the warehouse, so he could put on the special effects. Special effects he'd set up after Milo's genius started to show. And the lines Milo had started to cross.

Innocently of course. Yeah, right.

Just as he took the scrambled eggs off the heat, his comp buzzed.

He checked the message. The pod was en route. Good. "Milo, engage the privacy mode setting out front."

"Woohoo." Milo jumped up from the table and raced over to the control unit. "I never get to do this."

"Well, this time, it's necessary." He checked the digital readout on the screen. "Good, it's all working." He set the plate on a tray. "Take this to Lani. I have to accept the delivery."

Milo looked at him. "Are you sure about this?"

Liev stopped, handing Milo the tray. "It's a little late to be asking, isn't it?"

Milo's lively features twisted in regret. "I'm just realizing that this is all my fault."

Liev stared at him. "Really, just now?" He leaned on

the counter to stare at him. "You really don't get it, do you? This isn't some game. This isn't a rush to beat the technology. This isn't something you can just do, then forget about." His temper fired as he thought about all he had to deal with. "You have damaged lives—in ways we can't begin to know about. And you have ruined Lani's."

"I haven't ruined Lani's at all. Don't you see this is beautiful? She has a great life waiting for her here. We'll make it great."

"But you didn't give her any choice. You did this *to* her not *for* her. You made her a victim of your machinations. And that's just wrong. She should never have been brought into our world. You didn't ask her if she wanted this. You didn't care."

Liev stopped and stared, wondering what it would take to get through his brother's head. "What you did was wrong. On so many levels. And you've left me to deal with your mess again."

"She's not a mess. She's a miracle." Milo stepped in front of Liev. "Look. I'm sorry for the problems right now. I'm sorry for any that might still come, but, damn it, Liev, I did something that no one else has done." His eyes glittered with excitement. "Can't you see the greatness here?"

Liev choked. "And that's all this means to you, isn't it?" Would Milo ever see what he'd done? "And what about Lani? Do you think she'll consider this greatness?"

A buzzer sounded.

"Damn it. They're early. I hadn't expected them so fast." Liev raced to the door, leaving the food tray behind with Milo. Liev opened the door to see his delivery.

"Bring it in here." He stood by as the pod floated toward him. He led the way to where it would stay. He'd planned on getting one a year ago but had had a hard time with the registration requirements. "Thanks."

"No problem. You'll pay through the nose for this, but, hey, it's worthwhile."

"I hope so," he muttered. He took the paperwork, glanced at the bottom line, and said, "So we're good?"

"We are. As long as I get that software, we're done."

"It's already in progress." And it was. He smiled at the man who would prefer to not be named. Liev knew him vaguely. Liev had had to go to a friend of a friend to make this happen as it was. So he had taken his first step on the wild side. Then again, Milo had pushed them all over there already.

But Lani needed healing. Liev couldn't leave her like she was.

Speaking of which, he went through the simple process to open the pod and to check it over. "Lani," he called out loudly, "do you think you can walk over to me?"

He didn't hear an answer. He walked to her room to see her struggling to get out of bed. Just that much effort had her sweating. Damn Milo.

And she still wasn't fully dressed. He cursed himself for looking. As she struggled to tug the blanket around her shoulders, he cursed himself again for not taking a better look while he could.

He raced over. "Here. Let me help."

She gasped from the effort. "I thought I'd be fine. I got up on my own this morning." Her face flushed, then paled.

He frowned, hating that she was hurting. "And you will be fine again. Let's get you into the pod. That will help."

He half carried her to where the machine waited, then helped her lie down inside. The pod, once fired up, would read her statistics. That stage could take a while. Before shutting the lid, he glanced down at her, wondering what he'd forgotten. Mentally he went through the process from the previous night and brightened. "Right. The critter."

He ran back to her bedroom and winced. The cat didn't look very good at all. It only opened its eyes and stared at him, its huge golden eyes wells of deep dark pain. "I'm so sorry," he whispered. He scooped him up and carried him to Lani. She lay with her eyes closed, never moving as he approached.

Carefully he lay the critter on her stomach. On the shelf below the pod were several blankets. He picked one up, opened it and tucked it along her side. If she wanted it, she could easily pull it over her.

Her eyes flew open, saw her pet, then her gaze shot

up to stare at him in surprise.

He shrugged sheepishly. "He looked to be suffering too."

"He is," she whispered, her gaze gentling. She studied Liev's face and then smiled.

A real smile. No sarcasm, no anger, just a slow blossoming movement that he couldn't tear his gaze away from. And then the smile hit her eyes.

He was enthralled.

She might be mad sometimes, and she might be sarcastic, but now that she was smiling at him, he realized how honest she was. There was no artifice with her. Stretched out on a soft blanket in his new pod, she was a beautiful innocent to his world.

She was who she was, and to hell with what anyone thought of that.

He realized how unique she was. And how much he was falling for her—damn it. Milo had been right. He was interested.

Chapter 8

LANI SOAKED UP the warm healing rays. It was like lying in warm sunshine in a babbling creek as waves ... or something similar rippled over and under and maybe even through her. Whatever it was doing, she didn't ever want to leave because it felt that good. This pod was amazing. She needed one of her own. She'd skip the bed and sleep in this every night. She wanted to sleep now, but, at the same time, she didn't want to be unconscious and miss this experience. The only unsettling comparison was its coffin-like appearance. Yet there wasn't any sensation of being confined in any way. There was such a peaceful sensation to being in here, it soothed her emotions and thoughts.

Charming snoozed beside her. She wondered if he was worse off with this time-travel thing than she was.

At least she could talk and walk. Charming was more or less flat-out. She reached down and scratched the back of his head. He was definitely more laid-back right now. No nagging for attention. No nagging for food. And speaking of food—the pod had arrived before they could eat. Her stomach growled then silenced almost instantly. Was that the pod telling it to be quiet? Or was her body happy to accept this healing time right now knowing that food was coming?

She was more worried about Charming than she was about her own situation at the moment. Her heartstrings tugged at the thought of losing her best friend. She had nothing left of her old life but him. He'd been with her for four years and was a major part of her life. To see him hurting like this …

Charming raised his head and gave her a pitiful look. "Food?"

She smiled in relief. "There will be food soon."

He groaned. A long, slow, guttural sigh that made her laugh.

"I'm glad to hear you are feeling better."

"Feel awful," he whispered in a low throaty voice.

"I love how you can talk now." She tilted her head in thought and added, "It must be a side effect of the time-travel."

"I love how you can talk now, too," Charming mimicked. "It must be a side effect of the time-travel."

She gasped, then laughed and laughed. And maybe he was right. Maybe she'd been the one to learn to talk cat and not the other way around. But if that was the case Milo wouldn't have heard him either. And she needed Milo to have heard him so she didn't think she was crazy.

She relaxed, her hand resting on his ruff, letting the hum of the pod do its thing. Whatever that was. The lights were a soothing blue, and no computer voice disturbed her peace and quiet. Food and more coffee would be good, but, barring that miracle, for the moment, she was doing just fine.

She closed her eyes and fell asleep.

LIEV WALKED INTO the newly designated pod room and smiled. Both guests were sound asleep. The pod would work better, faster, if they stayed that way. At least until it did its job. Getting her healthy was just the first stage of this process. Time to work on the second.

He opened his comp and dialed a number that was likely to be a popular one for him over the next few days.

When a computerized voice answered, he read off a series of numbers he'd memorized. When a voice came on the other end, he stated, "I need an ID for one young female."

Silence.

Liev held his breath. There was no guarantee that he'd get his request fulfilled, but he didn't know where else to go. Lani needed a solid ID to go anywhere. And she needed to be tagged. Thankfully he and Milo made a lot of money because taking care of Lani would become a major expense.

"Anything else?"

"Yes." He winced. It was from here that things could get dicey. "I need a tagging completed."

The person on the other end sucked in his breath. But, when he spoke, his voice was calm. "That is an expensive process."

"I know."

"You have the funds?"

"I have the funds." There was no point in elaborating. They either believed him or they didn't. And he'd pay the price, regardless. He had no choice.

Silence.

He waited. If this person refused, it would be one person more who would know his secret. And such a secret would be dangerous, especially for Lani.

"When?"

"As fast as possible." Then he reconsidered. Maybe not so fast. Lani was still healing. He didn't want these people to know why she had no ID or tags. And they might if they saw her now. If it could be in a few days, that would give her longer to heal. He had no idea how long it would take, but she needed every day. He'd have to take her out of his place soon. But she needed to be strong enough to handle everything that was coming.

His world was not for the faint of heart.

"Tomorrow morning. No food or water for twelve hours prior."

And the voice rang off.

Liev stared at the comp in his hand. "That went well." Maybe. They didn't give him a price. They didn't ask for his address. They didn't ask for any medical details about who was being tagged. Would they contact him again or just show up on his doorstep?

He immediately removed all trace of the call, then just to be sure, destroyed the comp in his hand. He'd get another one from his home office later. Secrecy was paramount.

He walked to where Lani slept in the pod. The top was glass so he could see her inside. The critter stretched across her belly. She'd taken to the pod as if it were the answer to her prayers, and, given the fact that it was easing her pain, it probably was. Stunningly beautiful in sleep, Lani was both a problem and a gift. He stood, enjoying the sleeping beauty, when he realized he really didn't want to leave her. That, more than anything, sent him bolting from the room.

Back in the kitchen, he came face-to-face with Milo.

Milo, dark overtones in his young voice, asked, "Did I just hear you correctly?"

Liev's stomach sank. Milo would need to know eventually, but Liev didn't feel up to a fight now. "What did you hear?"

Milo looked around furtively. Liev rolled his eyes. "We're in our home. Stealth is on. No one can hear us."

"You can't be sure of that," Milo cried out. "What if someone has this place bugged?" He reached up to grab his colorful green mohawk with both hands.

Liev stared at his brother in disgust. "You care now?"

Round glazed eyes stared back at him. "You don't

understand. I can't have people knowing about her."

Liev narrowed his gaze. "Why?" he asked, his tone ominous.

Milo shifted uneasily. Not quite bouncing but neither did he stand steady. And that wasn't good.

"Milo, what are you talking about?"

He leaned forward. "It's my technology. My design. My invention."

"And?"

"And, if people find out, they will steal it." He wrung his hands.

"Damn it, Milo. This isn't about keeping your code secret. This is about a young woman whose life you destroyed. You do realize she could die, don't you?"

Milo stared in the direction of the healing pod. That he seemed to be considering the pros and cons of Lani's death pissed Liev off. His brother was naive and simpleminded over some things, other people's things, but he was also incredibly focused on his stuff.

"No," Liev snapped. "That is not a good outcome."

Milo slid him a sidelong glance. "I wasn't going to suggest we kill her, for God's sake, but if she should happen to die …"

"Which I'm trying my hardest to avoid happening, if you hadn't noticed." Liev strode to the liquor cabinet sunk into the wall. He couldn't believe the bizarre turn of their conversation. He poured himself a hefty whiskey and threw it back. He shuddered as the firewater coated his throat and prepared to do battle in his stomach. He had been doing this a lot lately.

"You really shouldn't drink that stuff. It's bad for you."

Liev choked. "You're worried about my health while you talk hopefully about Lani's death?"

Raising his hands in surrender, Milo snapped, "I'm just saying that, now that I know it works, she's the proof. If she dies, I'll still know that it works, but we won't have to deal with the evidence." He shrugged. "No biggie."

Liev poured a second shot and took a sip while he stared at his brother. Forced to question his kid brother's ethics, … his morals. His conscience. And that was an alarming step. He swirled the golden liquid in his glass. While Liev had been bending over backward to keep Lani safe and to make her as comfortable as possible, his brother had been contemplating the advantage of his experiment dying.

How did that work? In his world, not very well.

"Milo," he said in a deep hard voice, "I don't ever want this discussion to come up again."

His brother pouted.

That was the only description Liev could come up with. His brother was actually pouting. Again reminding him that, for all his genius, Milo essentially had the mind of a sixteen-year-old male trapped in a twenty-two-year-old body. Maybe one day the two would match up, but Liev hadn't seen any sign of the gap closing in years. Milo had hit sixteen with such enthusiasm; it was as if he'd found a way to not age again.

That concept startled him. If Milo had found a way to haul in some poor woman from a couple centuries ago, had he also found a way to slow or stop the aging process?

If so, if anyone found out, neither of them would ever be safe again.

CHAPTER 9

WHISPERED CONVERSATION SLIPPED under the edge of the pod's hum, disturbing her rest. Something about her dying? Really? Worriedly, her hand automatically searched for Charming, reassured to find his warm body snuggled up against her. He was still alive. She waited for his chest to rise with his next breath, then relaxed. Was she close to death? Or was that a hypothetical statement if the pod didn't do its job?

Dry-eyed, she studied the running green light shifting along the edge of the pod. Was she so badly damaged by Milo's experiment that she wouldn't survive? Assessing her own situation, she realized that, outside of a deep permeating fatigue, she didn't feel bad. Walking was a problem though. As if every step required too much effort, like she weighed hundreds of pounds more than she had before her time-travel trip.

That had to be due to the change in atmosphere or maybe gravity—as if she were living on Jupiter.

Only she wasn't. But time had obviously changed the atmosphere in the future. Or her body felt it had. Or maybe it was the oxygen levels? Were they different here? Was she at a much higher altitude than she thought? And maybe the why didn't matter. If she couldn't go back, she had no choice but to go forward. If she could ever get up.

She shifted her legs tentatively. They didn't ache the same as they had. So maybe the pod was doing its job. Her arms worked fine; her mind was clearer. She didn't know if she was supposed to live in here until she was fully healed—if such a thing was possible—or if there was a day-to-day booster thing going on.

She wasn't opposed to coming in here daily. She did feel better in the pod. Maybe it was a weaning-off thing. As she strengthened, she'd need it less. She was truly grateful they had such technology. Too bad she couldn't take a unit back home. The people there could use this.

And this time period needed better food. Her stomach growled again. It had been getting worse since she first woke up. She'd lost track of time and didn't know if it was day or night, and her stomach didn't care. It needed sustenance.

She pushed against the lid. Instantly it opened so she could see out but it kept working on her and Charming.

She glanced at the partially closed door where the voices drifted toward her. Were they still talking about her impending death? More likely she'd die from starvation at this rate. Should she search for food herself? And would she recognize it if she saw it? Or did the cupboards hold mostly shakes and boosters, like Milo had threatened?

That sent her stomach careening to almost heaving. Immediately the racing lights warmed and slowed. Probably in response to her discomfort. She closed her eyes. In truth, she didn't want to leave the pod. She was warm and comfortable and pain free. But very hungry.

"Liev?"

No answer. She called out louder. "Liev?"

Still no answer. Damn it.

She tried to push the top of the pod higher and found it wouldn't budge. Shit. Was she locked in here? It's as if it had opened enough for someone to check on her, talk to her but not enough to release her.

And, if so, how would she get out?

"It won't open unless it is done with its work." Liev stopped at the doorway. "Or, if you need to go to the bathroom or have another physical discomfort, it's set to automatically shut off when the patient has other needs that supersede the healing." He frowned. "But I can adjust the settings so you can open the lid just by pushing on it."

She stared at him. "The only body function that is paramount at the moment is my appetite. I'm incredibly hungry."

He approached the pod and pressed some buttons on the console. After a moment, he glanced down at her and said, "I raised the height of the lid so you can lie sideways easier." He stared at her. "I guess you didn't get anything to eat yet?"

"No." She gave him a tentative smile. "And, if possible, I'd really like to change that."

For the first time all day, a real smile lit his face. "I can do that." He winked at her in a surprise move that left her doubting what she'd seen.

She watched him leave, feeling happier than she remembered in a while. The resemblance was only a passing glimpse now to Lawrence. Liev was a different person. She no longer felt any animosity toward him. He wasn't responsible for this. She understood he was trying to help.

He was his own person, and she really wanted to know him better. He'd been nothing but kind to her and patient with his brother. There was something so very attractive about that kind of caring.

Being pampered like this was addictive.

But Milo? ... Now him, she wasn't so sure about.

As she came to terms with her new reality, she felt better emotionally. Sure, she'd lost so much, but maybe, just maybe, she'd also gained something.

According to Milo, her life as she'd known it hadn't ended up too special. As in, she'd never married, never had children, and she'd never had a major career that he could find.

That was quite depressing. She'd just been approved for a special Internet Security program at the company she'd worked for. She'd worked hard and had kept her head down at that company, making sure she did nothing to get into trouble. It had been gratifying to have them recognize her value – until she lost that opportunity, compliments of Milo. She couldn't even imagine what happened to all she'd left behind. Had her date shown up to think she was avoiding him? Would anyone call the police to say she was missing? Would her boss call her cellphone more than a few days before deciding she'd just quit?

Her furniture?

Her bank accounts?

Her car?

Would she end up forgotten, as a dusty missing person's file in the back of a rusty file cabinet? Or worse on the side of some old milk carton emblazoned with her face. Although she was pretty sure only missing children were put on milk cartons.

Bottom line, as far as anyone in her old life was concerned, she'd just upped and disappeared one day. And she had no way of changing that.

Thank heavens she had Charming with her when Milo decided to pull the trigger ... she couldn't imagine her poor pet behind left behind to fend for himself in a locked up apartment. It just brought back how completely selfish and inconsiderate Milo had been... in more ways than one.

If she could return to her own time, she'd try harder to make something of her life there. She'd like to think an event like this would be a wake up call to enjoy the time she had. But, if returning was no longer a possibility, she wanted to make the best of whatever life she had here.

Maybe she could make a success of it.

She didn't know how society worked here, but, with Milo and Liev around to help, maybe she could make a difference.

She'd overheard Liev say something about tagging. She didn't know what that meant, but—if it allowed her to be one of them with a proper ID—she was all for it.

She was so busy making plans that Charming had to forcefully let her know something was different.

He pushed himself up on his front paws, yelling, "Food!"

Lani struggled to get out of the pod. It seemed to resist her efforts at first; then, all of a sudden, the lock released, and it opened. She really didn't want the two men rushing in here to find Charming screaming like he was. But the poor thing did need a square meal. So did she.

When she stood on her feet, a chill settled in. Already? How did that work? She cast another glance at the pod. Charming had collapsed on the top of the blanket, and the most godawful sound came from his mouth.

"Food. *Fooooooood*," he moaned and rolled over sideways in a dramatic movement. He was proving to be a major prima donna.

"I'll see what I can find." She tugged the blanket

from the pod and wrapped it around her shoulders before she stumbled forward, her gait unsteady. She leaned against the wall and made her way to the unusual doorway. Tall, almost to the ceiling, the doorways were narrower than she was used to. The floor smoother as if made of glass. Maybe the people were skinnier today than in her time. Lord knows that would be an improvement.

She staggered into the next room, trying to sort out the layout. How had she gotten into this place? And where the heck was the kitchen? Her stomach growled loud enough that, if anyone was in the apartment, they'd hear her coming.

Good. She slipped her hand over the wall, but there was no light switch. "Of course. That would be too easy."

With one hand on the wall, she kept moving forward. The hallway opened up into a large spacious room. Something along the lines of a living room. There were several open sitting areas clustered together in little cozy conversation corners. Massive artwork was on the wall ... one appeared to stare at her. She quickly glanced at the rest of the living room.

"The big-ass living room," she muttered, staring around her in surprise. For some reason, she'd thought this apartment was tiny. She hadn't seen much of the apartment since she'd been here, but where was the damn bathroom again? Then she needed food. And so did Charming.

Slipping around the corner, she stopped. There was another bathroom. A monster-size room and different from the last one she'd used. She used it, then, after washing her hands, she stared into the mirror and shuddered. God, she looked pathetic. Even seeing that, she straightened her spine and tried to put a smile on her face. That looked better. She took a couple deep breaths and smacked her cheeks lightly to put some color on them. Having done what little she could, she opened the door and shrieked.

"Whoa. Take it easy." Liev reached out to stabilize her. "Come on. Let's get you back to the pod."

"I need clothes and food. And Charming needs his kind of food," she whispered. "I'm so hungry. He's going to be just as hungry if not more so. I normally feed him twice a day. And he gets dry food all day long in case he gets hungry."

"I'm preparing food. Wait a second." He disappeared, only to reappear with a long flowing robe. He quickly dropped it over her head flickering the blanket she wore away. Immediately her body warmed.

"Now, hold onto my arm, and I'll take you to the kitchen. After you eat, it's back into the pod."

"I do feel better and warmer. Thanks for the robe, it's lovely and cozy." She gave him a small apologetic smile. "I just feel much better."

"The pod will do its job, but it'll take some time. The robe will adjust to your body temperature and warm or cool you as needed. Give both time to work."

"Seriously? The robe is magic like the pod." She stumbled forward, every step a triumph. "At least I'm walking. Although very awkwardly. Like a day-old fawn…"

He laughed. "You're not that bad."

"I hope not but I doubt I'm much better." She managed a tiny chuckle. "Thanks for helping."

"Not an issue. I'm just sorry that you're hurting."

By the time he'd finished talking, he was helping her into a chair at a table. She stared around and realized the kitchen was more or less normal-looking. After Milo's talk about shakes and nutrients, she was scared to imagine what food Liev had come up with. "I'm just so hungry. I wonder if it's a side effect of the time-travel," she said.

"Maybe. You need food for healing." He opened a section of the wall before she had a chance to see what he'd done. "Is that a refrigerator?"

He turned to look at her. "It's a cooler. I'm not sure what a refrigerator is." He placed a clear plastic jug with eggs and something resembling cheese on the counter. Her mouth started watering. "Could I have a piece of cheese?" she asked, her voice faint with hunger.

He brought a thick slice over for her. As if he knew she had food, Charming meowed steadily from the back room. She winced, feeling guilty over her cheese. "Is there any chance you have something for him?"

He grimaced. "I don't have anything resembling cat food, but there is some ground chicken in here."

"Ha," she said. "He'd love that."

And he did.

Instead of taking the food to the pod, Liev brought Charming to the kitchen table. Charming howled pitifully the whole time. Once at the table, Lani wrapped her arms around him, trying to keep him calm until some food arrived. But he wouldn't be calmed. He definitely wasn't living up to his name.

Finally Liev brought a bowl of minced chicken over. "Will he eat it raw?"

"I think he'll eat your hand as well if you don't give that bowl to him."

Liev lowered the bowl, and Charming damn-near jumped into it. Lani was actually embarrassed. "Sorry, he's usually better mannered."

Charming stopped eating and turned to look at her. "Get over it. I'm hungry."

Her gaze whipped to Liev to see what he thought of her cat's speaking abilities. He took a step back. Then a second step and a third, until he'd come up against the counter. His gaze went from Charming to her and back again. His face flushed red then turned pasty white with shock. He swallowed loudly several times as he stared at Charming. "Did he just talk?"

"Oh, I'm so glad you and Milo can hear him too." She grinned happily. "I was afraid I was going nuts."

Liev stared at her in shock. "Are you serious?"

"Oh, I'm serious with being happy I'm not the only one who can hear him." She leaned forward and said in a conspiratorial whisper, "He's only been able to do this since Milo's little trip. This cat could never talk before."

Charming snorted and shook his head, spraying flecks of raw chicken across the table. "Yes, I could. You couldn't hear me."

She raised one eyebrow and stared at Liev. "Is that possible?"

"What? That the cat talks? Hell no." Liev shook his head rapidly back and forth all the while staring at Charming in fascination.

Little did he know. Lani grinned, enjoying herself. "No—that I'm the one who is different? And you two are more advanced? Maybe that's why you can hear him? Or did the trip through time make him able to speak?"

"Or both. If one of you has changed in such a major way, then it's quite likely that both have." He ran his hand through his hair, leaving it looking wonderfully tousled. And, damn, she wanted to run her hands through it too. Her stomach growled again.

And didn't Charming inhale his food faster, as if he thought she would get close and eat his food?

She leaned closer on purpose. "Hey. Don't worry. I won't be eating your chicken."

"Oh, crap." Liev straightened, staring at the eggs. "I forgot about your food." He exhaled sharply. "I'll make a cheese omelet." He grabbed a bowl and cracked two eggs. His movements smooth and practiced. She liked that about him. What he did he did well – at least the little she'd seen of him.

She coughed. "Uhm, I don't suppose you could make that a big omelet, could you?"

He raised his gaze to stare at her, as if asking if she was serious. At her hopeful look, he cracked two more eggs. "I think your eyes are bigger than your stomach."

"Not a problem. I'll help her." Charming sat on the table cleaning his paws. At the odd silence in the room, he looked up to find them both staring at him. "What? I'm still hungry."

While Liev whipped up an omelet—and she was amazed to know that they were still making omelets this far in the future—she found a cloth and wiped up her cat's mess. He'd been so hungry he'd inhaled the food with the end result he'd spread it everywhere.

At least it was real food she'd be eating. She had been afraid they'd replaced food with pills. And, to a certain extent, they might have. If she could take a pill and make her stomach feel like she'd eaten a roast chicken with all the trimmings, she'd swallow a half dozen of those pills and maybe feel like she was back to normal. Right now, her toes were so empty that she was pretty damn sure she wouldn't make the walk back to the pod. Charming was obviously no better as he eyed every move Liev made with in an intensity that almost laughable. And if she had any energy to laugh, she would.

Just when she thought she'd cry from hunger, a plate was placed in front of her. The aroma hit her nose making her moan in joy. It was rich, warm, and soooo fragrant. Melted cheese filled the inside of a golden omelet. She could taste it already. Cutting up a section into small bits to cool, she forked up the first bite and closed her eyes and moaned. "Oh, that's good."

She opened her eyes to find Charming whacking at the piece closest to him. He caught it in his paws and dragged his prize toward him.

"You get that piece because you got it covered in raw chicken, but that's it. No more."

Charming ignored her as he tried to eat it, but the piece was too hot. He meowed and batted the piece a couple times, then tried to bite it. Whining, he gobbled it down anyway.

"Geez. Aren't you full yet?"

Charming stared, his gaze never lifting from her plate. "I'm hungry."

"Oh, man." She cut him another piece and slid it toward him. "That's it. The rest is mine."

She wrapped her arm around the plate protectively. She glared Charming into backing up.

Liev laughed, a refreshing, open laugh.

Lani ignored him until she'd finished every piece of omelet on her plate. Unfortunately she was still hungry. She turned woeful eyes to Liev. He stared, switched his gaze to her empty plate, then back to her face. "Really?"

She nodded. At her side Charming meowed in agreement.

"Both of us are still hungry."

Blowing out his breath, he turned to his kitchen cabinets and brought out a loaf of thick crusty bread. Her eyes lit up at the sight of it. "Now that would be great. I love bread. Not sure how Charming feels about it."

"I've got cheese to go on this." He cut two thick slabs and brought it over for her, then went back for cheese and butter. She munched happily as Charming worked through a chunk of cheese. "That feels so much better," she said when she was done.

An odd sound rang through the apartment. She stiffened. It sounded like an alarm. "Is that a fire alarm or something?"

"I don't know what it is." With a sharp look in her direction, Liev said, "Stay here. I'll be right back."

He disappeared. Lani looked at Charming, but he'd taken off. She didn't blame him. Feeling scared and hating being alone in a place she knew nothing about, she retraced her steps to the healing pod as fast as she could. And, sure enough, she found Charming hiding between the folds of a blanket inside.

"Good idea. Maybe we can hide away in here until this calms down." The noise was horrific enough to hurt her ears while in the kitchen, but, as soon as she crawled inside the pod and closed the lid, the noise disappeared. "Oh, thank heavens," she murmured as the assault on her ears stopped. Just as she started to relax, the lid lifted. Milo, his face twisted with urgency, said, "Come. You have to leave. Now."

She was dragged out of the pod. At the last moment, she snatched up Charming before she was shoved ahead of Milo. "Where are we going?" she whispered. "I have no place to go."

"Liev has a place for you. Hurry."

Within minutes, she was hustled into a room she'd never seen before in one of those weird cubes she hated and spinning at a speed her body couldn't stand— upward.

"Where's Liev?" she asked angrily.

"He's coming." Milo chewed on his fingernail and shifted on his feet anxiously.

"Not good enough. If you think to dump me somewhere and hope I'll take care of myself, you're sad—"

"Lani. I'm here." Liev appeared on the other side of the glass. Then, while she watched, the glass between them disappeared. Damn, she wished she knew how that worked. "What is going on, Liev?"

"It's a security inspection. My system warns me when trouble is coming." He pushed her ahead of him. "Milo, go back and let them in. Be natural. I'll engage stealth on the pod and the apartment."

"Got it." Milo took off.

"I don't think I like your world," she said.

Liev tugged her forward, making her hurt as she tried to move faster than she could. "Stop pulling on me."

Spinning to face her, he stopped at the look on her

face. "Please hurry."

Looking at the worry in his face, she realized this was big. Dangerously big. If anything happened to separate her from Liev, she'd be lost. And with Charming having his unique ability to speak, ... he'd be taken away from her too.

Ignoring the pain, she started to run.

THANKFUL THAT LANI finally seemed to understand the urgency of the matter, Liev followed just slightly behind. He didn't want her to collapse when she ran out of energy. And, if she did, he wanted to be there to catch her.

The pod appeared to have been working as she held the pace steadily. He slipped past her to open a door. Inside was the rooftop elevator. With the three of them inside, he sent it to the top beside Johan's place. Liev kept a worried eye on Lani. She was breathing hard, and her color was pale, but she still stood.

Charming looked up at him. Liev glanced away, still not able to reconcile what he'd seen and heard. A talking cat. Holy crap. He couldn't even begin to think about the ramifications of that. If the cat talked as a result of the time-travel, Liev could just imagine what the scientists would say. And what they'd want to do to Lani's pet.

It would be disastrous for society at large.

And this feline gave him the creeps. Those huge golden eyes seemed to see into his soul. And who was to say the cat didn't? If it could talk, what else could it do? Liev shuddered inwardly. He really didn't want to know.

At the rooftop, he could hear loud music at Johan's. Should they blend into one of his constant parties or try for the private rooftop garden that, in theory, the others didn't know about? The only problem was that the garden was damn small. It was a space he used when he needed a few moments away from everything. It would be a tight squeeze for the two of them. And he was almost looking forward to that.

His gaze caught sight of Charming.

Okay, the three of them.

But, given the sudden raised voices at Johan's and the now silent music, Liev would take a squeeze over trouble. Lani couldn't be seen yet. He led the way quietly around the rooftop garden to the back maintenance section. Slipping around several large vents, he stepped out onto his tiny private deck.

Lani gasped and spun around. "Oh my! You can see the whole city from here."

He smiled. "Not quite. I do like to come up here though. It's pretty spectacular." Liev stood by Lani's side. "I guess this doesn't look like what you are used to?"

She stood, shocked, and stared out at the city. It was a replay of what she'd first seen after escaping the office. And more—so much more. Oddly shaped dome buildings that stretched out as far as she could see. Gemstone colors glowed off the sides of some walls with multiple green spots dotting the area ... And the air traffic? ... She shuddered at what appeared to be loads of air traffic. Her gaze flitted from one thing to another. "It's beautiful," she said, "but it's so, ... so ... foreign-looking."

"In what way?" Liev asked, looking at her.

"It's surreal, like a science fiction movie set. Foreign. Alien." She shifted Charming in her arms. "It's nothing like what I'd expected. Huge buildings in weird shapes and colors and lights. The way vehicles move. In my time we still drove on paved roads that were on the ground ..." She shrugged. "It's just so bizarre to think that I'm actually here."

Liev grinned. "It is. Don't tell Milo, but it's also great."

She stared at him. "We'll see. That he managed to do what he did is pretty amazing. I'm not sure I appreciate it still, but I do understand the genius required to make this happen."

Liev stood in front of Lani. "You aren't afraid of heights, are you?"

She shook her head. "I'm fine," she murmured. "It is pretty spectacular. Scary but beautiful."

"It is." He glanced around. "It's also private."

"I presume we're hiding here until it's safe to go home again?" At his nod, she rubbed her temple. "It's because of me, isn't it?"

"In a way. You don't have ID or tags. If anyone were to find out about you at this stage ..."

Liev hated to admit that the government was corrupt and getting worse every day. He'd love to reassure Lani that this world wasn't worse than the one she'd left. But it would be hard to find proof of that.

Still, her world wasn't perfect either. And, as long as one kept a low profile in his world, everything would be fine. Most people never had any run-ins with the authorities, and life continued in an easy way.

If Liev didn't have Milo to contend with, Liev's life probably would have been easy too.

"How long do you think it will take? I'm getting tired," she asked. And, for the first time since they arrived, he took a good look at her. She'd slumped against the wall, and her color had all but disappeared. She appeared to be doing a long slow slide to the ground. She pressed her lips together and shifted the huge cat in her arms again.

"Do you want to sit down?"

She looked around. "There isn't a place to, is there?"

"On the floor."

His comp emitted a *beep*. He pulled it out and smiled. "That's Milo. All clear. The suits came. They visited with him, asked a few questions, got a few answers, and now they've left." He smiled. "Hopefully satisfied enough that they won't be back."

Lani smiled. "Good. Let's go."

"Not so fast." Liev clicked through his comp, searching his security readouts to make sure his place was empty. It appeared to be. He did a search throughout the building. Checking for an anomaly, something else that was illegal. A few people were in the building, and, like Johan, most had secrets. Authorities were not welcome here. Liev checked his wrist unit. "This building is supposed to be exempt from those raids. Lord knows we pay enough for that, but we still seem to have one or two a year." He looked up. "Okay, it looks good."

"Going back the same way?" Lani asked, heading toward the corner.

"Yes, but slowly. Just in case."

They made their way back to the rooftop elevator. Loud music was once again blasting from Johan's place. If it weren't for Lani, Liev would suggest they blend into the festivities. But, with the cat and her current level of exhaustion, she'd stand out as new and different. It also wasn't safe to bring her into a social situation yet. She needed to learn more about this world.

Within seconds, they were in the elevator and scooting back to his floor. He led the way home, and, as soon as they were inside, he set up stealth mode again. As far as anyone outside this place would know, the place was empty. There would be no power readings, water usage, lights, or heat showing up on scans. It was about all he could do. And, considering Milo, it wasn't enough. But it was more than most had. Liev walked into the kitchen and set up the coffee. When he turned, two sets of eyes stared at him. Fatigue in both but also hope. He was stumped. He tilted his head and asked, "What do you want?"

Lani grimaced. Charming had no such problem stating his need. "*Foood.*"

CHAPTER 10

LANI WATCHED THE shock settle on Liev's face. "Sorry, but I'm hungry again too. All I want to do is eat and sleep."

He shook his head and motioned to the bread still on the table. "I have some cooked meat in here somewhere." He turned to rummage in the cooler.

After placing Charming on the kitchen table, back where he'd been sitting earlier, Lani picked up the knife and started cutting the bread. Milo walked into the kitchen and stared at her.

"See? I told you shakes would be better," Milo said. "Her body needs nutrients. She'll need a lot of food to make up for what she could get in a vitamin drink."

"If that's the case," Lani said, "a shake and food would work. Just a shake, no way."

Behind her, Liev said, "That's actually a good idea, Milo. Make them a booster. Get the data from the pod, and fix one for each."

Charming, staring at the bread in her hand as she buttered it, asked, "What's a booster?"

"A shot of vitamins in this case, to help your bodies adapt," Milo said.

"Ah. So food." Satisfied, he sat back and watched every move she made.

"If possible, Milo," Lani said, "could you make Charming a very small booster portion with cream as a base? He's not likely to drink anything else."

Charming nodded. "Cream. Cream is good."

"Cream is not good for you. It's fat. And not a good fat." Milo made a disgusted sound. "It's awful, and it will kill you." He stalked off in the direction of the pod.

Lani turned to look at Liev, who appeared to be slicing a hunk of meat. She just didn't know what kind it was. And she hated to ask. She was so hungry that, if it was cloned, she probably wouldn't care. Tomorrow was a different story. "Milo has strong views, doesn't he?"

Liev looked up with a smile. "Always has. Not to worry. He has a big weakness for chocolate." At her surprised look, Liev's grin widened. "Makes him seem more human, doesn't it?"

"What about your parents? Are they alive? Live close by?"

He stacked the meat up on a plate and brought it to the table. "They died when Milo was little. I've been looking after him for a long time."

"That must have been tough." She couldn't imagine. She'd had a hard enough time looking after herself. She'd had parents, though they'd never been close. And now … she stared down at her bread. She hadn't spoken to them in over five years. Would they even know she'd disappeared?

She asked, "Is there a way to research the people who lived in my time?"

"There is. The record-keeping of today is something quite different than in your time. So you'd need training, but we can certainly do that. You'll need to learn our way of life. In fact, I had considered taking you to Johan's while we were up top, but I figured you'd need to familiarize yourself a little more with our ways before socializing."

She stared at him. Took a bite of bread and meat and chewed. Her mind reeled with the implications of all she'd have to learn. The pitfalls waiting for her. She swallowed.

"I can't imagine." A shudder slipped down her spine. "It's hardly like visiting a foreign place."

"That's exactly what it is." He dropped a piece of meat in front of Charming to go with the other pieces already lined up. Charming showed no sign of slowing down or being distracted from his food. "You'll be fine. There are a lot of things to learn, but it could be worse."

She stopped and stared. "In what way?"

"We all speak English."

He had a point.

Milo returned with a large glass of something fuchsia pink and a small bowl of something much less bright. He placed the glass in front of her and set the cream in front of Charming.

Charming asked, "What is it?"

"Cream," Lani said helpfully. "Their version here. Try it. So far you've eaten everything else."

He sighed, leaned in, and sniffed. "Doesn't smell like cream."

Feeling like she was enticing a two-year-old to eat his spinach, she said, "It will be good. Besides, it's to make us feel better. To help us heal."

He looked over at her, his huge golden eyes staring at her, unblinking. "Then you try it."

She should have seen that one coming. Shooting Charming a disgusted look, she picked up her glass of pink drink, took a deep breath, and swallowed a big gulp. And felt her throat close and her eyes water. She gasped for a breath, desperate to keep her reaction minimal as Charming watched her with a smug look.

"It's different. Hot almost. Definitely different." She gave Charming an encouraging smile. "Try it."

"Yours is much stronger than his, as you are bigger, and the damage to your system is a little more extensive." Milo slumped at the far side of the table, a glass of something rich and creamy with a light green tinge to it in his hand. He held up his drink. "Mine is an everyday dose, whereas yours is intensive."

"I'll say," she muttered. With a grimace, she picked it up again. Resisting the urge to plug her nose so she couldn't taste the drink, she downed it in one gulp. It was the only way she would get it down. She just hoped it would stay there.

She placed the empty glass on the counter and gave Charming a fat grin. "Your turn."

He glared at her, then at her glass, before slowly approaching his bowl, nose first. He sniffed several times, then reached out and licked several times. And missed the cream each time.

"Oh, no, you don't. You drink it all up, just like I had to." And she hoped she'd never have to again. She leaned in closer and watched as Charming tried again. This time he got some of the pink stuff and froze. He licked his lips several times and said in surprise, "Hey, it's good." He lowered his head and lapped at the cream.

"Damn. How come his tastes decent, and mine is so strong I feel like puking?"

"Yours had to be stronger." Liev stood, walked to a cupboard, and pulled out a glass. He held it to a wall, and it filled automatically. She hadn't even noticed a spout. He brought it back to her. "Plain water."

She reached for it and drank the whole thing, then held it out, asking for more.

"Wow, she drinks like she eats. Told you she'd be perfect for you." Milo grinned up at his brother.

Liev quietly brought a second glass of water back to her. Then carried on out of the room.

She accepted it and turned to Milo. "Did I hear you right?" Lani asked, a new hardness, coldness in her voice.

Charming sat back and stared at Milo. "Ha. You are

so going to get it now."

Milo took another sip of his drink. He shrugged his shoulders nonchalantly. "What's the problem? I said he'd like you. So what's the big deal?"

She stood. "Did you actually go back in time ... to snag me ... for your brother?"

LIEV WAS ABOUT to join them again when he heard Lani's question. And he really wanted to hear his brother answer that. He stepped up to the doorway and listened.

Milo's face twisted at Lani's words, like he'd sucked on a grapefruit. Lani eyed him suspiciously. "You did, didn't you?"

He shrugged and stared at his drink.

"Why me?" It seemed that was the burning question in her mind. Like, how had he come to choose her? Then it was a good question. Liev wanted to know the answer too. His brother had gone to a lot of trouble but why her?

"I had to find a target, ... er, ... a person to use for the experiment. Liev has horrible taste in women." He gave an exaggerated shudder and a quick sidelong glance at his brother. "So I figured I could do two things at once. Find a lovely woman for him, add a few enhancements, and try out my experiment at the same time."

Liev winced. Is that what Milo thought of his girl-friends? While he mulled over the pathetic state of affairs, Lani spoke up.

"Enhancements?" she asked in a low dark tone of voice.

Milo shrugged. "That part didn't work out the way I expected it to."

"In what way?" Liev spoke from the doorway. It was the first he'd heard anything about enhancements. "What did you do? You never mentioned enhancements before. What kind of enhancements?"

"Hey." Milo held out his hands defensively. "I was just enhancing her communication abilities."

Liev stared at him in shock. "Why?"

"Because you're deep, man. You like to talk. You like to communicate. I figured, if she wasn't much of a communicator, that could be easily enhanced."

Somewhere in the background, as Liev tried to work his way through the maze of thoughts crowding his brain, he heard laughter. As in maniacal, off-the-wall laughter. He stared at Lani.

She was bent over, and damned if tears weren't roll-ing down her cheeks.

Liev waited. Charming reached out and smacked her with a paw. She appeared to slow down after that. Finally she choked back the last of her giggles.

"Care to explain?" Liev asked.

She took a deep sobering breath, wiped her eyes, and pointed at Charming. "Milo's enhancement did work. It worked on Charming. He's the one who got the gift of communication. He can talk now…" She giggled again. "Thank God, Milo didn't add bigger boobs or something just as ridiculous. Imagine how Charming would look then."

"Really?" Charming sniffed the air. "That would be preposterous."

The two men stared at her, then at Charming.

"You were supposed to come alone," Milo said slowly, staring in fascination at the cat. He opened his mouth, as if to add something, then closed it, and just shook his head. "And I thought that enhancement was minor for your body size, but if they, … it …" he corrected quickly, catching Liev's attention for a moment, adding, "went to him, … considering *his* size, … it would almost make sense." He slumped down on the closest chair. "Wow. Just like, … wow."

There was a long silence while everyone stared at Charming.

He preened.

Lani couldn't believe it.

"Those must be some enhancements," she murmured.

He wondered briefly what the enhancements would have done for her. Then again there was no going back to find out. He then returned his attention to Milo. "There are a couple other problems with your logic."

Milo raised an eyebrow.

"Of course there are." Lani shook her head, her face

twisting in disbelief, as if overwhelmed at the casualness of his actions. "First off, what if you did choose the perfect partner for Liev and destroyed her in the process?"

Milo blinked.

She snorted.

Such a thought hadn't even occurred to Liev. And he didn't want to consider it now. "Did you even think about failure?"

Milo laughed. "No. Nothing is a failure in life. There are just times where I've learned something didn't work. And, if this didn't work, no one would know. You'd have just been vaporized or something."

"And what if only half of me made it?" She felt sick inside. "What if, only from the belly up, I lay in a gory pool of blood on your floor?" she asked in an ominous voice.

Milo's skin took on a greenish tinge. Then his lips twitched. "Nah. It was either all of you or none of you."

"And how could you know I wasn't some serial killer you were bringing for your brother?"

He grinned. "We have all kinds of DNA markers for that sort of thing. Serial killer material you're not. You actually pick up spiders and put them outside so they don't die."

She frowned, a little weirded out that he knew that about her. "But I won't touch them with my hands."

He laughed at that. "See? That's perfect. Caring but careful."

"And a personality profile?" she asked. "No way you could have done one of those on me. Not when I lived hundreds of years ago."

"We have advanced profile markers for many traits today. Sure, it was a gamble, but you had the same general look that Liev loved, and you fit the other parameters I needed, so it was a good gamble." He straightened. "And you're here all in one piece, so it's time to move on."

Move on? What did that mean? She tilted her head. "Move on?"

"Time to adjust. Time to adapt. Time to deal." Milo leveled a look her way. "This is your life now."

He turned and sauntered in that casual no responsibility, no regret manner of his.

Liev moved closer noting the pale color of her skin, the slight stoop to her shoulders. "Time to go back into the pod. Tomorrow could be stressful."

"More than my life already is?" She made a choked sound half laughter and half protest. But her gaze stared up at him hoping he'd brush it off as a minor visit.

He couldn't lie to her. Tomorrow was important and likely to be difficult. "Unfortunately"—his face turned grim—"yes."

CHAPTER 11

B ACK IN THE pod, the lid closed encasing the two of them in warm healing waves, Lani and Charming slept, woke, and slept some more. When Liev walked in the next morning, she felt much better. Until he said her specialist was here. He dropped a stack of clothes on the bed and walked out.

Like, what the hell was a specialist here? It's not like he said what kind of specialist. And why was he *hers*?

She frowned at Liev's retreating back but struggled upright, gasping at the lingering aches and pains. She hated to leave the warm coziness of the pod but it's not as if Liev had given her a choice. She was sure if she didn't get out, he'd return and help her out himself.

"I'll be there in a minute," she called out as she stumbled to the bathroom. She took a few precious moments to wash up and try to run her fingers through her hair. Once back into her room, she dressed in the unusual but cool clothing. That they fit like a glove was a little disconcerting. How had Liev known her size? Still, they looked good on her. She smoothed her fingers over the silky black material of the cropped top, loving the exotic feel. It met the half skirt along the back of the shorts and it was like nothing she'd ever seen before. Then neither were the interesting gemlike diamonds decorating the top. The shorts were knee length and were closer to capri leggings if she wanted something to compare them too. The skirt went down her legs but only along the back and sides. And the material ... she'd never felt anything like it before.

Liev had left two small pieces of material that looked like ballet slippers but again so soft she didn't know if they were meant to wear outside or were meant as slippers only. She slipped her foot into the first one and moaned as it wrapped about her foot in a warm soft yet perfect fitting slipper. Smiling in delight she slipped the other midnight blue slipper on, realizing they matched her clothing. Did everything here match naturally? Could the colors of the clothing change? 'Cause now that would be beyond cool.

She made her way down the hallway, doing a quick twirl to watch the skirt flare out. Nice. She grinned. Not only that, she was grateful that, although hungry, she didn't feel like she would die anytime soon. Staying in the pod appeared to be the best answer. Besides it had become a warm nest she felt safe in. Too bad she had to leave it now.

She walked into the kitchen. As she caught sight of the stranger, her breath lodged at the back of her throat, her steps slowing. Two hundred years into the future made no difference here. There was a specific look to those who walked the shady side of life. A thinness to his lips and thickness to his brow, but it was that flat gaze that clinched it.

Not saying anything, he motioned at her to sit down. She glanced at Liev, uncertain. Immediately he stepped closer and motioned to the chair, a gentle smile on his face. "Sit, Lani. It will be over in a moment."

Uncertain but willing, she took her place. And waited. Behind her, the specialist unpacked a bag and lay items out on the counter.

She looked at Liev and whispered, "Will it hurt?"

He shrugged, his gaze on the man behind her. "Maybe a little. You can go back into the pod afterward."

Lani twisted around, but the specialist showed no signs of hearing their conversation. Considering he hadn't said a word yet, he might be a deaf mute. She turned back and waited.

She shifted restlessly when nothing happened after several moments. She twisted around again to see what the stranger was doing, but this time Liev stepped in her line of sight. She glared at him. Just then the specialist stepped forward and grabbed her arm. He searched the soft tissue above her wrist, the rough skin of his fingers almost scratching hers. After a moment, he dropped her hand and checked the other one.

She frowned. "Anything wrong?"

He never said a word and just returned behind her. She opened her mouth to speak again when Liev picked up her hand and pressed her fingers into the same place on his wrist. And she felt some hard material inside.

Her gaze widened in fear as she understood. This specialist now knew she didn't have one. Her mouth fell open, and she leaned in close. "But now he knows."

Liev nodded, bent lower, and, with his lips against her ears, murmured, "He's here to give you one."

"But isn't that dangerous? For you?"

"More for you. Don't say anything more to him. Cry if you need to. The pod will fix any damage afterward."

"Oh, God, it'll hurt, won't it?" And her heart started to race. She clenched her fists. She was such a baby with pain. Tears burned in the back of her eyes. She couldn't do this.

As if understanding, Liev crouched down beside her, wrapped an arm around her shoulders and squeezed gently. "Easy."

She swallowed hard. She had no choice. She had to have whatever that thing was that Liev had. She couldn't even ask for details without letting the specialist know the extent of her ignorance. And that would only bring more questions. And more problems. She hated the subterfuge, the necessary lies. She'd never been at any good at those. She'd be sure to mess up one time.

Not to mention the way words tended to blurt from her mouth without warning.

Liev massaged her shoulders, making her realize she'd frozen in place, her muscles locking down.

Just when the wait seemed interminable, the specialist walked over again—holding a gun of some kind in his hands. She gasped in shock, and Liev gripped her shoulders—not quite forcing her to stay in place but letting her know he could if needed.

She didn't want to watch what happened so she kept her gaze forward. The stranger snagged her arm and turned her hand palm up.

Something cold was placed against her skin.

She closed her eyes and held her breath.

There was a hard pinch, then nothing. She frowned. Was that it? All that worry over nothing. Just as the thought filtered through her brain, her head lolled to one side, and she blacked out.

LIEV LET HIS breath escape slowly when Lani's head drooped to the side.

"Hold her still," the stranger snapped.

Liev grabbed her shoulders to stop her from slumping in the chair, then slid his arm under her head, his other arm wrapping around her ribs to hold her still. "I've got her. Go ahead."

The specialist nodded and proceeded to do the quick laser surgery to open her wrist. Liev knew he was taking a chance doing this. At birth, newborns were tagged within the first hour of life. When they hit sixteen, the tags were switched to the ones they'd have for the rest of their lives.

At birth, it was easier as the bones and tissues were soft, pliant. The initial tags were easily replaced as the body was already well accustomed to their presence. Lani had never had a foreign object implanted under her skin, as her computer scan had confirmed at Johan's place. Her nerves were fully grown. Any damage at this stage and she could lose the use of her hand. Scar tissue was yet another problem. He could only hope to get this over with and to get her back into the pod quickly. It should mitigate the damage to this morning's surgery—if nothing went majorly wrong.

He watched the man work fast and efficiently. When Lani's wrist was opened, Liev had to look away. There was little blood with the high-intensity laser but holy crap … He gritted his teeth, and, unable to help himself, he dropped a kiss on her head. After another long moment, he risked a second look at the surgery, relieved to see the tag lying nestled in her muscles. The blood loss was minimal so hopefully the after effects would be too. He could only wonder how her body would adapt to such a thing at her age. His society had been using ID implants for a long time. They appeared to be the answer. They couldn't be lost, transferred, or stolen. When surgically removed from the body, an alert was automatically sent to the Registrar.

"Will this work?" Liev asked. At least the specialist appeared to be competent.

He nodded. "Should."

"It's registered?" He couldn't help asking questions. If this didn't work, Lani's life was in danger. And that was unacceptable.

The specialist nodded again. "It is. When I get this closed up, I'll start the programming."

Ah. Right. The whole computer world that his society ran off of. Lani had to be included, or else she'd always be an outsider. A fugitive. And that would be very difficult. Fringe groups were in his world, as have been in every century. They lived free of the government restrictions and regulations but barely eked out a living, always on the run from the military. He sighed, staring at the gentle soul in his arms. She didn't deserve that. She didn't deserve any of this. She'd been the innocent victim in all of this, and honestly she'd taken what had happened with a grace that continually surprised him. He didn't think he'd be as half as accepting if he'd gone through what she had.

"Done."

Liev looked up, relief flooding through him. "Are you?" He studied Lani's wrist. The laser had closed the wound. It was red and puffy but surprisingly healthy looking. The man waved a healing wand over it, and that improved the look of the skin again. Liev exhaled. "Will she be in pain when she wakes up?"

The specialist shrugged. "It's possible. The body needs time to adapt. Her wrist will ache. The fingers could go numb off and on and could potentially swell."

All things the pod could help her with, so it was

minor in the scheme of things that could go wrong. The specialist stood and collected his instruments. He repacked his bag, then opened a side pouch, and removed a comp unlike anything Liev had seen before. The man pulled a chair forward and sat down. Using an odd-looking antenna, he angled the comp so it faced Lani's wrist. He clicked a few buttons, and a series of lights under her skin lit up. Liev's eyebrows shot up. He hadn't realized how much programming went into this.

But the stranger seemed to relax into his chair now that he realized the system was active. He bent his head and worked his thumbs on the keyboard. The lights on Lani's wrist continued to beep and flash, then settled down to a steady pulse.

Liev looked at his own wrist. There were no lights. No beeps. Not now. But, if he bought anything, a series of lights appeared at his wrist as the exchange system went through its security checks. He wondered how long this would take and how much information he'd need to give to make Lani a history. She had to have a full background for the databases to be happy.

He waited quietly for the stranger to work.

The man looked up. "Her name?"

"Lani Summerland."

The stranger keyed it in. Without looking up, he asked for her birth date.

Doing the math quickly from the little he knew, Liev picked July first, twenty-four years earlier.

There were several other questions, like gender,

which he could easily answer. Then came the harder ones. Family history. He stalled. He could give Lani's real parents' names. He'd seen their names in Milo's file, but he had no dates for them. He gave up their names willingly enough and waited, hoping more wasn't required.

"We'll put down that the records were destroyed in the Felonia Crash, shall we?"

Relief washed through Liev. So much information had been lost in that disaster. It was the perfect answer. And he realized that excuse had likely saved a lot of people. No records meant create your own and that was exactly what he needed to do right now. "That works."

The specialist switched to a series of questions about her medical history. He, of course, had no idea, but the pods hadn't found anything major, so he presumed she had none. At least as far as the database was concerned, she was incredibly healthy.

He had no idea what other information was being placed in Lani's fake background. And he didn't care as long as it was neutral and wouldn't raise any flags if checked. She needed to have flaws, just not big ones.

A few more questions followed about her education and schools. Not knowing many, he used the same schools that he'd gone to and gave her a degree in IT systems. At least he could train her for that. And, since so many people had a similar education, it was a common course for her to have completed.

Then finally it was done. Lani was a single orphaned female, twenty-four, educated, healthy.

The specialist said, "Last section. We have to connect to her financial information."

Liev nodded, ready for this. Last night, when he realized what this process would mean, he'd opened some accounts under Lani's name. He punched in his access code on his comp, then brought up the account. With a few swift clicks, Lani was connected to the credit system of his times to her implant. He'd transferred a moderate chunk of money to help her get established but not enough to raise any alarms. He had no idea what she would need over the next year, and he knew he'd use what money he had to make her life as good as he could make it.

That was the least he could do.

But she'd need so much more. He couldn't even think of how much she had to learn. She was going to need special training to understand their technological world. She'd need history lessons so she could even hold a conversation with others and not give herself away. And that was just the tip of the iceberg. She had a million minefields yawning under her – their – feet.

The specialist packed up the comp and closed his bag. He turned to Liev and held out a porter. Liev stilled. This would be the first time he would see the price for Lani's tagging. He reached for it, took a look, schooled his features to not react, then held the unit to his own wrist and pushed the buttons, allowing the payment from his account. He wanted to laugh at the mockery of the company name on the specialist's bill. Liev had just paid for cosmetic upgrades for Lani. How true. It would be hard to consider any other body modification that would match this expense.

When it was completed, he handed the unit back to the specialist, who nodded, put it in his pocket, and proceeded to walk out of the apartment.

Feeling odd, yet relieved about the whole thing, Liev reengaged stealth mode on the apartment. A part of him wondered if he wouldn't be better off relocating so as not to be found again.

He'd paid the bill. But he'd also opened himself to potential blackmail in the future. And Lani, now safe from the government, was in danger from the very men who'd helped save her. There was one other thing he could do to protect her—but it was a last resort. And it would involve his family. He wasn't quite ready for that step yet.

His mind raced for ways to protect them both. She moaned just then, and he realized she needed the pod. He could work out the rest of the details later. Surely Milo could find something on these men to help balance the scales.

When both sides had secrets to hide, the playing field was leveled.

And that would be best.

But first he had to see to Lani's care.

CHAPTER 12

LANI WOKE TO tears rolling down her cheeks. She tried to swipe them away and cried out, instinctively cradling her sore hand to her chest. It took her moment to settle the pain and realize she was being carried in strong arms again. A protective and caring set of arms. Liev.

"Easy, Lani. It's over." Liev's comforting voice washed over her.

She tried to understand what was going on. Liev was speaking, but she didn't understand what he was saying.

"I'm taking you back to the pod. After an hour in there, you'll feel much better."

The pod. Healing. Her sore wrist.

Then her memories came rushing back. That stranger—her specialist—and him picking up her wrist. She didn't know what he did to her but whatever it was had knocked her out. Or ... she'd passed out. That would be a bit much as she'd never fainted in her life. Considering the pain she was currently in, major fainting had been the easy answer.

For some reason, this injury, this injustice was done

in an attempt to make everything right ... had become the last straw.

Maybe because she was tired, maybe because she hurt so, and maybe it was just because it had all become too much, but, once she started crying, she couldn't stop the tears.

"It'll be all right, Lani," Liev's worried voice whispered in her ear. "I'm so sorry we had to do this."

"It's all right," she sobbed as the tears poured out. "It's not your fault."

"And yet it is." He sighed as they entered the pod room. "Milo is my brother, and he brought you here for me. I certainly didn't ask him to do this, but, because of his actions, your life has been ruined."

They entered the small room and he shifted her in his arms. He laid her down in the pod. She moaned as her wrist was jostled.

"I'm so sorry," Liev said. The pain in his voice was so evident that she wanted to reassure him it was fine—only it wasn't fine. Her wrist throbbed with pain such as she had never felt before. Charming meowed and shifted to lie at her feet. She wiggled her toes against his thick fur, loving that he was here with her.

"I am too," she whispered, lying back and shuddering. "I had no idea it would hurt this much."

"It shouldn't," Liev said quietly. "He gave you something for the pain, but I'm not sure your body can handle the drugs of today."

Not a nice thought. She wasn't sure she could handle much of his world that she'd seen so far. "The pod might help." She curled into a ball, her injured arm lying on her side so that the pod's rays could gain clear access. She closed her eyes, tears still leaking through and took several calming breaths.

"I'll go mix a pain cocktail." He lowered the pod lid. "I'll be back in a moment."

She could hear his footsteps retreating. Thank God. She was set to have a royal bawl but hadn't wanted to while in his arms. She'd been holding back, but, now that she was alone, the sobs rolled free. Everything hurt, and it seemed like her life was the absolute worst it could be. She cried and cried, letting the tears and the stress and the pain drain from her overwhelmed system.

She'd always been proud of her ability to adapt. Her ability to stand up tall and weather the storms around her with grace and acceptance. She wasn't sure she could in this situation. She would try hard, but, damn, this was a mind-bender to set anyone off-balance. Oddly enough, by the time she stopped bawling, she felt better. Just to let go like that had helped her ease back the stress levels.

Sure, her wrist still hurt, but the coiled sense of being too full, too hurt, too ... whatever, was gone. She let the last of the sobs hiccup out before she took several deep breaths.

"Are you okay now?"

Liev's worried voice came from the open doorway.

Damn. She sniffled back the last bit of the tears.

"Sorry," she whispered, her voice thick and ragged, still clogged with tears. She knew her face would be red and puffy. She could only hope he didn't open the pod. She didn't want him to see her this way.

At the reminder of the pod, she brightened. Maybe it could heal her puffiness at the same time as it worked to heal the time-travel damage. She turned slightly so her face was directly under the pod's flashing lights. She didn't know if it made a difference, but her skin immediately started to lose the tight hot sensation.

"Don't be." Liev stood there beside her and lifted the pod's lid. "You've been through a lot."

She rolled her face into the blanket. It was an instinctive, yet childish reaction.

"Hey, don't do that," he whispered softly. "You don't ever need to hide from me."

That surprised a laugh out of her. "Sorry, I just know what I look like after I've been crying."

"Crying is a great way to release all that pent-up emotion. If anyone has the right to feel overwhelmed, it's you." He smiled down at her. "Give yourself a break. I think you've done wonderfully well."

In a surprising move, he lay down beside her in the pod and tugged her into his arms. Was he for real? Could any guy be this good? Or was it the men of this century? Because, if so, then wow!

And inexplicably, his acceptance brought on more waterworks.

Through her gentle sobs, Lani heard Liev's distressed voice. "Please don't cry, Lani. We'll make it work out. I'm so sorry Milo did this, but I promise, ... I'll do what I can to make it as good as I can. This really is a wondrous time to be alive. There are so many marvelous things I want to show you."

He kept talking and murmuring gently as if the sheer mass of words would help calm her down.

It was working. She wiped her eyes, surprised to find the pod had adapted its size to accommodate the two of them. Truly many innovative things were here. And somehow Charming had taken the opportunity to leave. And maybe it was time she stopped being such a wet dishrag and realized what an opportunity she had.

"I'm sorry," she whispered, though he'd told her not to be sorry. "I don't normally cry like this."

"It's like the physical effect on your body. There has to be some kind of emotional reaction too. Tears only make sense." He smiled at her. And damn if she wasn't starting to like that smile. A little too much. He had wormed his way into her heart. She really wanted him in her life.

She snuggled in closer and sighed happily. Maybe life wasn't so rotten after all.

He dropped a kiss on the top of her head. She smiled. He really was a protector. Another kiss landed on her side of her head. She shifted slightly at the same time he slid down a little, and she found herself staring into his eyes. Huge, deeply magnetic purple eyes. Like, how could that be? She so wanted eyes like that. Just gazing into them made her insides melt.

A tiny sigh escaped. He was so damn beautiful.

His eyes darkened.

She caught her breath.

Then he lowered his head ... and kissed her.

THE SWEETNESS OF her lips disarmed him and made the next kiss inevitable. His lips moved gently on hers. Tasting, exploring, feeling a response that set his pulse pounding. He deepened the kiss, needing more. Needing to know she wanted more.

That she wanted him.

Like he wanted her. He couldn't believe how much. He hadn't even known of her existence a few days ago, and it galled him to think his brother had found her and had retrieved her for him. Even worse to know that Milo had been right—she did look perfect for him—at least at first glance.

She twisted beneath him, her feet sliding up his calf, hooking under his pant leg and stroking his skin. He shuddered, sliding his hand around her back and down across her bare midriff. He'd chosen the clothes without realizing how sexy they'd look on her. Small and delicate, the clothing looked like they'd been created with her in mind. Add her almost ash-blond hair, and she looked like a slave girl from centuries ago.

He paused. She *was* from centuries ago.

She moved, twisting her body until his hand rested just below her chest. His breath caught in the back of his throat. As if his hand had a life of its own, his long fingers smoothed upward to cover her small rounded breast.

She gasped and arched into his hand.

He bent his head and lapped at the pouting nipple through the soft-as-silk material.

Her moan turned to a groan, and she shuddered.

God, he shouldn't be doing this.

It wasn't fair.

She needed to heal.

She didn't know what she was doing.

She couldn't know what she was doing.

She was dependent on him.

It was too fast.

She needed more time.

Argh. He pulled back, panting. "No," he groaned in a harsh whisper. "You're hurt."

"I'm hurting," she corrected. "And it'll hurt more if you don't kiss me again."

He raised himself higher so he could look into her blue eyes. "Are you sure?"

Her gaze widened. "I get that you're thinking of me. Giving me a chance to change my mind. But ..." She arched her back, brushing her breasts sinuously against his chest. "Unless you've done away with sex in your time ..."

"Lord, no." His voice was filled with desire, and he

lowered his head again. This time, he held nothing back. He wanted her, and he wanted her to know how much. All the reasons why this wasn't a good idea no longer mattered.

He wanted to show her how much he cared. To show her how good this could be between them. Instead it seemed like his fingers were all thumbs, and his normal suave skill had taken a hike. He was considered a skilled lover. But today, with her, it mattered too much, and he couldn't seem to get it right. And she didn't appear to notice.

He was all heat. Animal passion. And raw need.

He couldn't get enough of her.

Chapter 13

L ANI COULDN'T THINK. She didn't want to try. Sensations rolled through her, lighting nerve endings, sparking a hunger she hadn't expected. Her body shifted restlessly, rolling from side to side, following his touch. Needing his touch, needing his kisses, needing ... everything.

"Lani? Are you sure?"

She stilled. Her eyelids drifted open, the haze of desire parting just enough for a little comprehension to slip in. She stared up into his deep purple eyes. She wanted him. Did it matter that she barely knew him? Not right now. Did it matter the circumstances of how they came together? Not when she already knew him better than she'd known his ancestor.

Liev had shown heart in a tough situation. He came from a position of caring. He'd shelled out a lot of money to help her, and he'd been looking after his incorrigible brother since forever.

She'd enjoy getting to know him better, but she already knew everything that counted.

She felt him pull back, withdrawing. Shit, she'd taken too long.

"Yes," she whispered, her gaze deepening. "I'm sure."

He stilled, then shifted, searching her eyes. Whatever he saw made his own warm, deepen. He smiled tenderly. "Good."

And he lowered his head. This time nothing was hesitant about his touch. He stroked her breasts, cupping them to explore their weight, brushing the hard pebbles with his thumb. As she shivered uncontrollably beneath him, he learned her body with sure strokes, stopping when something fascinated him before carrying on to the next spot. She cried out, wanting the same freedom to touch him, but every time she reached for him, he shifted back or did something else to drive her crazy.

"Just lie back. Relax," he whispered.

"Only if I get my turn later," she murmured.

Deep dark laughter filled the pod as he said, "My pleasure."

She smiled and stretched out beneath him, her arms above her head, letting him do as he will.

And he took full advantage. He slipped her top over her head to toss on the floor beside them. His breath caught in the back of his throat as he stared down at her breasts.

She gave a catlike smile and arched upward.

He bent to take one pouting nipple into his mouth and suckled.

A deep, pulling sensation started in her lower belly.

Liev stroked down her ribs to rest at her tiny waist, his fingers flaring out to wrap around the swell of her hips.

She felt a shudder run through him. Lifting one foot, she stroked up and down his leg. "Aren't you wearing a few too many clothes for this activity?"

A wicked grin crossed his features. He slipped out from under the pod lid and stripped efficiently. She watched as his shirt went flying to the left, and his pants and boxers dropped—oh, nice—where he stood. If he had socks on, she didn't know or care. She was fascinated as he stood proudly in front of her, fully erect.

She pushed the lid of the pod up higher and patted the bed beside her. Instead he leaned over, slipped his fingers under the waistband of her half-shorts, half-skirt ensemble, and slowly removed everything, even her panties.

She lay under the glowing pod's healing rays and stretched under his heated gaze. While he stared, she whispered, "Are you planning on just looking?" Her voice husky and deep. "Or will you join me again?"

He walked to the end of the bed, grabbed her ankles, and gave a tug. She slid, legs open, all the way down until the heart of her was pressed up against him, with her legs wrapped around his hips.

She laughed. "Nice."

He grinned and tugged her upright until she was seated. She wrapped her arms around his neck and kissed him. His lips opened, his tongue wrangling softly with hers.

Swiftly he built up the heat between them, his hands restlessly stroking her body while his tongue drove her crazy. He slipped his hands down to her hips and held her firm.

And plunged deep into her center.

She gasped and arched. Shifting to ease the unexpected fullness, she wrapped her legs around his waist and tightened her inner muscles.

It was his turn to groan. Slowly he withdrew, paused, only to plunge back in deeper. He ground his hips tightly against her for a long moment, then started to move. His rhythm took over her thoughts and mind as he drove her quickly to the edge.

She cried out, "Liev!"

"I'm here. Fly with me." He grabbed her hands and stretched them above her head again. He kissed her hard and plunged inside once more.

His guttural groan sounded above her. Then a kaleidoscope of sensations exploded inside her, overwhelming and filling her, but still, something wouldn't let her fly free. An edgy nervousness rippled through her.

Liev's hand slid across her palm to entwine with her fingers.

She was no longer alone.

And they flew off the edge together.

LIEV PULLED LANI close to his heart. He could only hope this had been the right thing to do. He didn't want her to regret this step in their relationship. In fact, he wanted to love her all over again. And wasn't that a word to scare any single male?

Lani nuzzled against him and gave a happy sigh.

He cuddled her closer. "Are you okay?"

"Better than okay. I'm also not sore. Making love in a healing pod—unique concept."

That startled a laugh out of him. "Thanks. Spur of the moment and all that."

"Spontaneity is good for the soul," she murmured sleepily.

"Do you want to stay here and sleep longer?" he asked against her ear.

Her arms squeezed tight. "Only if you stay too."

"I will until you fall asleep." He shifted down slightly, grabbed the sliver of the blanket hanging off the edge, and wrapped it around her. "Just sleep."

She gave a deep sigh and closed her eyes. She fell asleep almost instantly.

Liev relaxed beside her, a slumberous warmth in his heart. It had been a long time since he'd held a woman like this. Sex, sure, but not the wonderful aftermath that came from making love with someone special.

"Liev," Milo called through the intercom that piped through their home, interrupting Liev's sated mood. "I think we may have more company coming. They just left the office after serving a warrant there."

Liev froze. "Friendlies or unfriendlies?"

"Unfriendlies."

Liev rolled over. "I'm coming. Make sure stealth is on."

He dressed quickly, his mind twisting with possibilities. "What now?" he whispered into the silence. Lani didn't need any more trouble—and neither did he. He just wanted time to spend with her. To get to know her without all the stress in their lives. And ... time to spend making love with her.

Instead he had to handle yet another headache. He dressed quickly, his movements controlled and efficient.

"Milo, did we get a notification that they were raiding the office?"

"About an hour ago. But, ... er, ..." Milo snickered. "You were busy, ... so you probably didn't get the messages."

"And you didn't interrupt me for something as important as a raid?" he asked incredulously.

Milo's voice dipped in embarrassment. "Yeah, I was a little involved in my VR unit at the same time."

"Damn it. Not the best timing." He could hardly blame Milo. This time.

He walked out to the kitchen and opened his scanner. When the pod had first been delivered, he'd placed it into a stealth container so that any scanners from outside the building could not see inside. That would keep the pod and Lani secret. This room and the pod had another layer of stealth coverings. He'd have to bring her out of hiding at some point, but hopefully not until she was ready. His comp jangled. He opened the screen to find the Council henchmen once again at his door. His heart sank.

Liev walked over and opened the door. "Good morning, gentlemen. This is becoming a habit."

The guard held up a red comp unit.

Shit. His nerves tightened. A court order. "I presume that's for searching the premises?" He reached for the unit, read the details, and sighed heavily. "Of course it is." He stepped aside while clicking through the screen, checking to see what the orders covered. "You're looking for the source of a power surge? In my home?"

"That is correct."

Hard to believe they had secured a warrant based only on suspicion. Liev shook his head and leaned against the door. "Go for it. Although maybe you could explain to me why this supposed power surge is of interest. It's not like they don't happen many times a month."

"The Council is concerned that your brother Milo may be up to his usual tricks."

As if. Liev snorted. "Only he doesn't work at home."

At least he didn't normally. In fact, right now, Milo appeared to be putting on coffee. Good. They would all need it when this was done.

"We checked your office building already and couldn't find the power issue there." He nodded at the techs doing a quick search of the home. "This is just to follow up."

"Okay." Liev waited with casual nonchalance. Deep inside, his head was screaming with warnings. Had they found anything at the office? Was there anything to find here? He'd been so careful, but it was easy to slip up on the little things. Damn Milo for missing that transmission. Instantly he kicked himself. He'd been just as absent as Milo. That he couldn't regret. But seriously, the timing sucked.

After ten minutes, the techs all filed out, shaking their heads.

"Are you satisfied?"

The guard nodded. "We will continue searching the other residences." He motioned to the team. "Johan Strand's place is next."

"Wait, what?" Liev asked. "Why would he have something to do with the power surge? And I thought you were searching to see if Milo had something to do with it."

"We had to eliminate any chance of Milo's involvement first." He turned and walked away, presumably to go to Johan's place.

Undecided on his next course of action, Liev realized he should warn his friend, but, at the same time, the guards could find out Liev had contacted Johan, and that could implicate both of them. Again. Liev couldn't risk placing Lani in trouble.

He closed the door and reset the security before

leaning against the front door. "Shit." He closed his eyes, sorting out what had just happened.

"Yeah, more trouble. All brought on by your brother."

"Whoa." Liev turned to see Charming, cleaning his paw on the chair nearby. "That's not true. Besides, you don't know anything about it."

Charming looked up, smiled, and said, "Really? Which part?"

"It doesn't matter. I'm not arguing with a cat." Liev walked past him.

"No, you'd rather mess around with Lani, I suppose."

Liev froze. Not so much that the cat was talking or even at his words. No, it was the edge to the cat's voice. Like an older brother looking out for his younger sister. A younger sister Liev had been caught dallying with. As if the relationship was wrong—at least to Charming. He even felt heat crawl up his throat. "Are you saying Lani isn't allowed to have a special friend?"

"Is that what you are?"

The cat's tone of voice was anything but friendly. Liev looked around, hoping for some help, but Lani was sleeping and Milo, per Milo's usual behavior, had taken off. Probably gone to his bedroom. Cornered, Liev tried to think of a way out of this conversation. Then decided on the truth. "I'd like to think so," he said quietly.

Charming stared at him intently, that gaze locked

on Liev's, searching, as if the cat could see into the heart of Liev. Then Charming dropped his gaze and shot one leg into the air and started to clean it.

"Umm …" Liev wasn't sure, but he would assume that he'd passed a test of some kind. He backed up quietly. Thankfully Charming didn't appear to notice. Liev checked on Lani, happy to see her sleeping soundly, and made his way into the kitchen. He contacted Johan on what Liev considered his secure line. *Need to get Milo to do his magic on that security feature too.*

Johan's face came on screen. Liev could only see gray walls behind his friend but had no idea where he was—except that he was not at home. "Are you okay?" Liev asked.

"Fine. I've secured this line, which will erase this conversation from any database. So speak freely."

"The guards just left my place. They're looking for the source of the latest power surge."

"I'm on the move. I slipped out the back and escaped." He grinned. "The guards said they were there to confiscate the pod—and anything else they deemed necessary. Or at least they are trying to. I have the pod set to self-destruct, … so, if you hear an explosion …" Johan walked forward, the scene behind his head shifting with his every step. "They will find some stuff. Although not what they are expecting."

Johan laughed, but there was a nasty edge to it. "Take care of your woman, Liev. I don't know where she came from, but you need to stop the Council from finding out about her."

Liev winced. "What do you know?"

"Not much, except from the pod. Also, I recognized your first visitor this morning from the rooftop cameras when I did a quick check around." He sighed. "Look. We live like we do for a reason. We have secrets. Protect yours. I'll take a trip. I may be gone for a while."

As Liev watched, he could see the scenery shift over and over behind his friend. "And a final word to the wise. The tagging, the unregistered pod, anything else you might think you've done to protect her, it won't be enough. You have to give her the protection of your name." His voice deepened. "Power needs more power, or you won't survive."

And he clicked off with a mock salute.

A heavy rumble carried overhead. That was likely the pod doing its self-destruct thing. Shit. Did it blow up in time, or did the Council henchmen get the information they were looking for? And, if they had, what recourse was there at this point? Liev's mind flipped to the other shocking point. Johan knew about Lani's tagging? That wasn't good. If Johan knew, who else could find out just as easily?

Liev's mind raced from one possible problem to another.

What Johan had said was true. Liev belonged to a long, powerful family line. And that was one thing the Council couldn't squash. Although his parents were dead, his uncles had kept him and Milo relatively protected for decades. Liev tried to be as independent as possible. Milo had pushed the limit, but, in a world where applications had to be made and accepted for children to exist, they were treasured. And families stood strong.

Powerful families stood for and against the government. He'd been trying to keep his brother out of any government involvement, and so far that had worked, but Johan was right. The easiest way to protect Lani was to enfold her in the family.

If she lived with anyone but Liev and Milo, she'd barely be of interest and could likely live out the rest of her life without raising any flags. But being here with them …

So the easiest answer was to set her up elsewhere away from them. Away from Liev. And that he couldn't do. Wouldn't do. Refused to do.

He'd done the best he could with Lani's fake background, but how would it hold up under closer scrutiny?

Therefore, only one option remained. If he'd had two minutes to think, he'd have realized it himself.

He had to marry her.

CHAPTER 14

LANI WOKE TO the sounds of an argument. She was deliciously warm, her body limber and relaxed. In fact, she felt pretty darn good. Even her wrist. She lifted it and rotated her hand experimentally. A low-level ache set in, but it wasn't bad. She ran her fingers across her skin and pressed gently. The ache deepened, but, considering what surgery had been done, it looked and felt amazing. She rolled over and shrieked in surprise. Charming was sitting inches from her face, staring at her with an odd look in his gaze.

"Damn it, Charming. Why are you sitting here, staring at me like that?"

His whiskers quivered, but he stayed quiet.

She frowned, reaching up to stroke his back. "Charming, are you okay?"

"Yes." He paused, then leaned closer. "Are you?"

She frowned. "Yes, I'm feeling much better." She held out her wrist. "See? I'm chipped now." She laughed. "Stupid, huh?"

"He's not Lawrence," Charming said, "but how do you know he's not *like* Lawrence?"

Heat rose on her cheeks. It was stupid to be embarrassed. Charming was a cat. What did he know about relationships?

Charming snorted. "It's not been so long that my old tomcat self doesn't recognize another tomcat catting around."

She winced at that. "I know he's not. I'm not trying to relive a dream," she said earnestly. "By the time my relationship with Lawrence was over, he wasn't the same man he'd been in the beginning."

"Lawrence was always the same. You just finally opened your eyes and saw him."

Wisdom. From a cat. Wow. It would take some doing to get used to this. She tried again. "You're right. But Liev is hardly the same type of man."

"And yet …"

She stiffened. "What's your problem with me having a relationship with Liev? Cat relationships last all of ten minutes."

"Except with you."

She smiled and reached for his chin to give him a good neck scratch. Charming was as insecure in this new world as she was. A relationship with Liev would put her baby's nose out of joint even more. His eyes crossed in joy as she continued to pet him. Seconds later, his engine started up. She lay here, rubbing Charming and thinking about her convoluted relationship with Liev.

Milo raced into the pod room. "You have to get dressed. We all have to appear in front of the Council."

And he bolted away.

Fear stabbed her stomach. She curled up into a small ball. Oh, no. She couldn't do this. But she had no choice, did she?

Charming spoke up abruptly. "Remember how you always dreamed about marriage and kids one day?"

She looked at him. "Yes?"

"Well, you just might be in for a surprise." And he hopped down and stalked stiff-legged to the doorway, his tail upright and waving in the air. He turned to look back at her. "Remember to keep your dreams fluid."

And he left.

Even more concerned now, she got dressed and made her way to the kitchen. Liev stood there, talking in a low voice to Milo.

"What's going on?"

Liev spun, smiled at her, and took a deep breath. "The first night you were here, I took you to Johan's pod. I tried to erase the information, but it caused some issues on the machine and sent corrupted data to the Council. Johan had some of the information still in the unit. When he was raided this morning, the Council gained access to the bulk of his place. He's gone traveling to avoid the Council. He had his own reasons for not wanting the Council to gain access to his place."

She shook her head, her heart calming slightly. "So we're safe?"

"No. In fact, only one way will ensure that you are safe." He paused.

Milo spoke up. "Make sure you know what you are doing, Liev."

Liev spun on him, his anger turning his face red. "You brought this on. Not me. Not Lani. Yet we are the ones taking the hit."

"You don't have to. We can find another solution."

"Really?" Liev asked, bitterness in his voice. "You've had time to utilize that magnificent brain of yours. What solution did you come up with?"

Milo looked downcast. She almost believed him. "Sorry, bro. I hadn't thought this through far enough."

"Yes, that's exactly right." Liev stood glaring at his brother and didn't look like he was prepared to stop any time soon.

"Stop the sibling stuff and one of you explain what does this have to do with me?" Lani crossed her arms over her chest, wishing they'd get to the point. "Milo said something about having to appear in front of the Council?"

"Yes. The occupants of my residence have been ordered to appear. The Council already suspects three of us are here. Therefore, the three of us will show up. It also means they'll know that you were the one in the pod." He paused. "The thing is, I don't think you are ready. Not for the Council. You could get into trouble over too many pitfalls there. You don't know anything about our way of life. About the government rules and laws we live with."

"But there is no other option, is there?" She studied

his face, even as her stomach sank. In fact, panic settled in on the edge of her consciousness. "I'm hoping there is though, as I really don't want to go if I don't have to."

Milo nodded. Liev said, "My family is wealthy, powerful, and we have members in big business across most sectors."

She waited.

"With all the problems, ... past, present, and potential ones racing towards us ..." He took a deep breath. "The best way I can protect you is to give you the benefit of my name. I can stand before the Council on your behalf that way." He paused, then added, "There is only one way to do that."

Her heart stopped. What did that mean?

"Lani, will you marry me?"

LIEV HELD HIS breath. Inside, he wanted to wrap her up and rush her to the opposite end of the planet. Only that would just delay the same ending. They'd be found. There was no way they wouldn't. But she looked so lost. So forlorn. It broke his heart.

He walked over and tugged her into his arms. He didn't love her yet, but he knew he was well on his way to that state. But she hadn't had a chance. Not to understand life here. Not to understand her options. Not to understand what any of this meant.

"I just want to go home," she whispered, her words a dagger to his heart.

Charming hopped up onto the table and whispered, "Me too."

"I'm sorry," Liev said to them both. "That's the one thing we can't do for you."

"Well, at least not yet," Milo said. "I might be able to build a new program, but they took most of my computer equipment from the office during the raid. It will take years to recreate my work."

"Do they know what they have?" she asked, peering around Liev's shoulder at his brother.

Milo shook his head vigorously. "No, the program was set to corrupt when anyone else accessed it. My records show it's gone."

She stared at him suspiciously. "And you didn't have a backup? A half-dozen backups? Some modern way to make sure you didn't lose everything?"

He gave her a sheepish grin. "I do, but it's not that simple. It's in pieces, and everything is encrypted." He frowned. "Chances are I could put it together again, but knowing that it succeeded and that they are now looking at it, makes me less likely to even try. It could take years to make it functional. Even worse, there's no way to test if it works." He glared at Lani in a challenging manner. "Do you want to try it under those circumstances?"

She shifted her gaze to Liev. "I have to make a decision today?"

Liev winced. "We have to be at the Council in an hour."

She stared at him. "And what? We'll tell the Council that we are engaged?"

Charming snorted. "Engaged? You?"

Milo and Liev looked at each other. Milo grinned. "Nope. You'll be married." He started to laugh.

Liev growled, "Milo, stop."

But Milo laughed louder. Between his giggles, he said, "Except for the final formality, you're already married. He just didn't bother asking you."

CHAPTER 15

L ANI STARED AT the two men. One howling with ill-placed humor, oh-so typical of a teenager. And the other shuffling uneasily on his feet.

Charming, his eyes bright and lively, stayed quiet, watchful. Smart.

"Are we married?" she asked in an ominous voice. Could something like that really have happened without her permission or her knowledge? Of course it could. These two could do anything.

She studied Liev's stance. She didn't believe he'd done it for a bad reason. After all, he could marry anyone. Why her? Unless he cared about trying to keep her safe. Of course, keeping her safe also meant keeping his brother safe—so that made a kind of sense.

But that was the last reason she wanted to get married. All she had ever wanted was to be loved. For herself. Not because she was a problem to be fixed.

She gazed at the window, realizing it was uncovered. She wasn't sure she wanted to look beyond this apartment. To see what was outside. She'd loved the bit from the rooftop space, but she knew more would be out there. She'd wanted to stay inside and to avoid the reality check of her new ... reality. She was in hiding, like a victim. And she was damn tired of feeling that way.

Ignoring the two men, she walked to the window and stared out. Even though she'd seen little bits and pieces before, she almost turned around and ran back to the healing pod. With no frame of reference for what she would see outside, the thought of going out there terrified her. The odd-shaped buildings appeared even closer from here. More alien in shapes and colors. And ... the flying cars—if they were flying at all, which they weren't—at least not in any way she understood flying. The cars had no wings. They all proceeded in an orderly fashion—at breakneck speeds!

A shiver ran through her. She'd seen this all before. Something about this time ... brought the reality of her situation closer to home. It had been fun, maybe getting to the point of being exciting. But now that she had to appear in front of the Council, ... everything was suddenly magnified. This was not her world. She didn't belong here. She spun around and closed her eyes.

No way could she go out there.

She could hardly breathe. She gasped for breath.

Liev rushed over. "Easy, Lani. Take it easy. It's not that bad."

Her head shook, and the words wouldn't come. She pointed out the window. He winced and pressed a button. Instantly the light in the room darkened, as if he'd closed the curtains. Only she had heard no *whoosh* of material sliding across the window or the blinds dropping. There were so many things she didn't understand here. So many things that worked in ways she'd never seen before. Her gaze landed on Charming. Were there other pets here? Cats specifically? Dogs? Were they allowed to keep pets in this century or was that joy gone? Yet Liev seemed to be more worried about her than Charming. As if Charming was a non-issue.

Something that would horrify him.

"I'm sorry. This is just the same view that you saw on the rooftop garden." He reached out to rub her shoulder. "The blinds have been closed for the last few days. Milo opened them this morning."

"It's one thing to see *that*, out there, when I'm safe in here, but to know that I will be forced to go into that world, ... to face the Council, ... it is not easy to be so detached."

"I hate the darkened room," Milo said cheerfully. "Felt like we were living in a prison."

His high-pitched voice paired with his words made her turn her head and stare at him. His bright purple air boots shone weirdly in the half light. She wondered if he was as harmless as he liked to appear. She hoped so. He could do a lot of harm to her if he chose. She gazed at Liev. He glared at his brother, obviously disliking his word choices. Then again, so did she.

She asked Liev quietly, "Are we already married?"

"Not fully. I need your acceptance."

"But the preparation, the paperwork, the legalities?"

"All done."

She shook her head. "When did you do this?"

"This morning," he said quietly. "After I realized it was the only answer."

"After the raid." She nodded, starting to understand. "After the Council went to Johan's."

"I called Johan to warn him, but he had already slipped away. He told me about the possibility that the Council may have some information that I didn't want them to have."

"Why would your name protect me?" She shook her head. "That makes no sense."

"Only because you don't understand how our government works today. We can protect you. But I need the family to help. Once you're family, they will surround you. Shield you. You can have me represent you in front of the Council as your legal partner. I already have the papers drawn up. Then you'll be safe."

The thought of leaving the safety of the apartment made her feel faint. The thought of facing the Council brought on nausea. She couldn't face strangers. Not now. Not yet. Maybe never. She shuddered inwardly. She studied Liev's serious face. "And will you be safe too?"

"Yes. We will be too." He nodded.

"Then your logic is flawed. Because, if that were the case, you'd be protected now. You two already have the family name."

Milo snorted. "She's got you there."

"No. She doesn't understand." He shot an exasperated look at his brother before turning to face Lani. "The family has been protecting us. But, at the same time, Milo keeps crossing the line. This time, there is more than just us at stake. I couldn't live with myself if anything happened to you. When the family closes ranks around you, we can make all this go away."

"You hope ..."

A weird musical sound filled the air. Liev looked frustrated for a moment. He ran his fingers through his hair. "It's time."

"Time for what?" Lani asked, looking around for the source of the music.

"Time for you to say yes or no." He took a step toward her. "Please, say yes."

She stared at him, confused, but realizing that he wanted—needed—the process finalized before she showed up at the Council. Something that mattered to keep her safe. To keep him and Milo safe. She didn't care about Milo, but she didn't want anything to happen to Liev. She hadn't known him long, but what she did know, she liked—a lot. She could fall in love with him. But that could only happen if she agreed to his plan. A plan that was deeply uncertain. But what were her choices?

None.

Damn.

"Answer one question first." She couldn't get over

the feeling that she didn't know something here. Something they weren't coming clean about. And she needed them to. "Why me? I understand that stuff about picking me because I fit the parameters. But there had to have been thousands of other women who would do."

Milo laughed. "I can tell you the truth about that now that you're almost family." He pointed at Liev. "My big brother here carries around a picture of a woman. I saw it a long time ago and asked him about it. It's originally from our family archives." Milo's grin widened. "He told me that he didn't know why, but something about the woman's smile struck him as special."

She turned to stare at Liev.

Milo beamed. "Show her, Liev."

Lani walked closer. "May I see it?"

Liev frowned, then reluctantly pulled a square metal-looking thing from his pocket. He unfolded it several times before handing it over.

She gasped. "Where did you get this?"

"I told you," Milo said. "From the family archives."

Lani stared at the very same picture she'd ripped into little pieces and had tossed into the garbage—or would be the same image except that the part with Lawrence had been cut away, leaving just a shot of her face. She couldn't believe what she was looking at. Coincidence? Fate? Destiny?

How much had her life changed in what? One day?

Two days? She couldn't tell anymore.

She lifted her stunned gaze to Milo. "Based on this one photo, you brought me here?"

"That image was the start of my research. I ran the tests, probabilities, scans, more tests—and you passed—so I figured, why not do something for my brother who's always doing nice things for me?" He patted Liev on the shoulder, then turned to address Lani. "You were meant to be a gift for Liev."

Bells chimed again.

Liev looked at her, his voice low, urgent, as he said, "Lani?"

Her gaze went from one brother to the other. Liev had taken the first step with the photo.

Milo the next.

This step was hers to take.

She swallowed, held out her hand, and said, "Yes, Liev. I will marry you."

And Charming, who'd been silent up until now, added, "Well it's about time ..."

This concludes Book 1 of Broken Protocols:
Cat's Meow.
Read the first chapter of Book 2 of Broken Protocols:
Cat's Pajamas below.

Broken Protocols: Cat's Pajamas (Book #2)
Chapter 1

MARRIED? TO LIEV Blackburn? Just like that? Lani Summerland's sense of humor kicked in. How typical of her crazy life. She couldn't find a man on her own in her twenty-first-century world, but was already married after a couple days in the twenty-third century. That was some matchmaking trick.

And not by choice.

Well, technically that wasn't true. The marriage part was by choice. At least it seemed like a great idea at the time. All of five minutes ago.

Lani Summerland stared suspiciously at the odd-looking adornment on her finger. It looked like a ring. It didn't feel like one. In fact, it had almost no weight to it at all. And, given the size of the deep purple rock on top, she thought she'd have noticed. Even the metal was soft, comfortable to wear.

She held her fingers splayed wide and shifted her hand in the age-old movement of women ever since rings were invented.

"Is it all right?" Liev Blackburn, her new husband,

and yet still a stranger in many ways, stepped a little closer to her. The clear glass cube, or what stood in for an elevator of this time period was almost normal—but there was no way she'd become accustomed to it as it disappeared into thin air when they arrived at their destination. Not to mention it didn't follow normal pathways or tracks. In fact, it went where it was ordered to go by an invisible technology all its own.

She flashed him a quick grin. "Sure. I'm just not used to wearing big rocks that appear to be made of nothing or that adjust automatically to any size."

"It's the new alloys," Milo, Liev's brainy younger brother, piped up. "Gold fell from grace when the shortage came about ninety years ago. This was the answer. It's no different than the clothing you are wearing. It adjusts naturally to the size of the wearer."

Well, that explained the perfect fitting clothing she wore that never constrained or tugged at her or pinched her skin. Amazing. "And the supersize rocks?" she asked, playing with the rock to make it twinkle in the light.

"Most are synthetic." Milo judged his brother in a joking manner. "But not this one."

She frowned, pretty sure that the rocks in her day came in a synthetic variation as well. But they still had weight.

Then she had no time to wonder as they arrived at their destination. Her heart beat faster as she realized this was it. "Now remember. Just smile," Liev said.

"Hold out your arm when requested to do so, but don't say a word unless asked a question." He shoved his arm outward to demonstrate.

She imitated his actions.

With a nod, he said, "If anyone asks where you're from, tell them you're from Felonia, and you arrived a couple days ago."

"Felonia," she repeated dutifully, dread congealing into a nasty ball in her stomach at the thought of anyone speaking to her. "Are you sure I can't just go home?" And back to Charming, who was even now resting in the pod at Liev's place.

"I wish you could. But, after this, no one will question your presence or your absence in the future." Liev wrapped an arm around her shoulder and led her forward. For all appearances, he looked like the doting new bridegroom. She shivered inwardly at the remembered passion they'd shared. Now if only they could head off on a romantic honeymoon.

But apparently not. She managed a warm glowing smile. He was her lifeline right now. And had quickly become the love of her life.

And, for that, she'd even put up with his brother Milo. Whom she had yet to forgive for dragging her into this century. Using an amazingly advanced computer program, he'd gone back in time, snatched her up, and brought her here as a gift for his brother, Liev.

Talk about a mind-bender.

That he'd also brought Charming and had accidentally enhanced his communication abilities, which were originally intended for her, was beyond anything she could have imagined.

The cube disappeared, and Liev, his arm still wrapped around her, led her forward into a large room with a clerk standing at the ready. "Good morning. Lani Summerland Blackburn," Liev said, "Liev Blackburn, and Milo Blackburn reporting in as requested."

The clerk frowned. "Only your presence was requested. Not your brother." He glanced up, saw Lani, and his frown deepened. "Not your girlfriend."

Lani straightened in outrage. Liev squeezed her shoulders. "My wife and brother are here because everyone living in my house was requested to attend."

"Wife?" Now the clerk's frown deepened. He clicked madly away on his weird tablet computer. Lani couldn't help but be fascinated as the lights flashed and pages shifted in a wildly erratic pattern she suspected was anything but erratic. She'd always loved computers. She hoped that she'd learn how these worked soon.

"Why do I have no record of that? I should have been notified." His voice rose slightly.

Control freak much? Lani eased out a shaky breath, trying to appear natural. As if showing up before a futuristic Council to answer for something she had nothing to do with was completely normal. She'd wanted to bring Charming with her for comfort, but both brothers had shot down that idea instantly.

Charming hadn't liked the idea much either.

"Nope, this is a human thing. I'm going to do the cat thing and sleep the time away. Have fun though and ta ta till later." And he'd walked away from them, head held high, his tail straight in the air and the tip flicking in their direction.

Even now she wanted to go back and hug him. He was her only link to her old life. Then he'd always been special to her. The two of them only had each other for years. Now it seemed their family had unexpectedly grown.

The clerk finally looked up and studied her. Whatever he saw made his lips curl. "Don't tell me. She's from the outer areas. From a fringe group."

Cutting words bubbled up on Lani's tongue, but she bit them back. She had no idea what the *outer areas* meant, but she didn't deserve to be treated as a lesser person because of it.

Liev nodded comfortably. "She is."

The clerk rolled his eyes. "Whatever. I'll put her down."

Liev nodded his thanks politely and led Lani into a huge chamber room where the ceiling appeared so high up she couldn't see the top. "Wait here. I shouldn't be long."

She reacted instinctively, reaching out to grab his hand. "Are you sure you can't sit here beside me?"

He leaned over and dropped a kiss on her forehead. "You'll be fine." He looked up and nodded his head at someone. "Here's my lawyer. Hahn Driscoll."

Lani turned as the stranger approached. He wore a uniquely tailored suit in glowing blue patterns. The styles might not have changed a lot, but the colors of today sure had. She smiled a polite greeting and shook his hand, charmed at the old-style greeting.

"Liev. Are you ready?"

Liev nodded. "I was just settling Lani here, where she'd be comfortable."

Hahn smiled at her, and damn if one of his teeth didn't wink out at her in the same color as his suit. Wow. Tooth jewelry. Her gaze widened, and her breath caught in the back of her throat. It was all she could do to not say something. Instead, she turned to look around her to see the room filling up. Several people took seats. She decided the best thing was to do the same. She watched one man sit down on a black pole that instantly widened to accommodate his butt.

Taking a deep breath, she promptly sat down on the closest pole, her breath whooshing out when it opened successfully into a seat to support her butt. Thank heavens. She took a shaky breath and smiled up at the brothers. "Go on. I'll be fine."

Milo gave her a weird finger salute she guesstimated meant something similar to *Right on* and turned and bounced forward. He'd certainly dressed up for the occasion, wearing a black-and-white striped skin suit. She shuddered at the jailbird look. It didn't matter how long she lived here; she would never wear a skin suit like that.

As if understanding her thoughts, Liev bent over and whispered, "You'd look better in that than he does." He kissed her cheek, winked at her, and walked away.

The lawyer, thankfully not sporting painted-on skin pants, waited a few steps ahead for Liev to catch up. Heads bent deep in discussion, they strode out of the room.

And left her alone.

LEAVING LANI IN the waiting room was one of the hardest things Liev had ever done. She knew no one, knew nothing about the world she found herself in, or the pitfalls that awaited her every time she opened her mouth to speak. But he had no choice. He quickened his pace to catch up to Milo, who was strolling on ahead. His brother's flagrant disregard for the rules had put them in this situation. Only Liev had compounded the situation by using his friend's healing pod to help repair the damage done to Lani and Charming from time-traveling.

Liev could only hope that his friend's attempt to destroy the pod Liev had used to heal Lani in would make today's Council visit more of a maintenance checkup than an actual investigation. He'd had his lawyer meet them here just in case, but Liev hadn't had time to brief Hahn.

The legal fees that his company paid to keep Hahn's

law firm available for times like this were exorbitant. As they were checked at the door and led into a smaller chamber, Liev spotted his old friend Stephen Cavendish on the Council dais. Relief swelled inside Liev. This might have started as a witch hunt, but it wouldn't end up that way. Stephen, young, only a junior Council member, was on Liev's side when it came to government meddling. And played the game well.

Liev smiled at his friend, relaxing even more when Stephen winked at him. This would be just fine.

Stephen opened the discussion. "I hear congratulations are in order, Liev?"

Liev beamed. "They are, indeed."

Milo bobbed at his side, his headset in his ear. He rarely spoke at these meetings. Probably just as well. What came out of his mouth usually didn't bode well for Liev or Milo.

In a genial let's-get-this-over-with-so-I-can-get-back-to-my-honeymoon tone of voice, Liev asked, "What is the problem that you needed to disturb me during my time of celebration?" He kept his face curious but amiable—at least he hoped it was. One sign of fear and these vultures would pounce.

"It's your friend Johan Strand," said one of the senior Council members. "He's wanted by the Council. When his request to appear was ignored, a team was sent to retrieve him. Unfortunately he'd set up some self-detonation on several of his equipment centers. Suspicious behavior at best." Some of the Council members nodded. "As your residence is known to be associated with him, we requested everyone there to appear here for questioning."

That's not quite the way Liev understood events to have gone down, but it wouldn't be the first time that the Council had twisted things to suit themselves. "First, Johan is an acquaintance, not a friend," Liev said in a what-has-this-got-to-do-with-me voice. "Second, I don't know anything about his equipment. Nor do I know where he is, if that is what you are looking to me for answers about." He stood tall and straight. "And my wife knows even less."

The Council stared at him. Even Stephen. Then again, Liev had always been good at playing the Council game.

Liev waited patiently. Ever since Milo had gotten them in hot water a year ago, whenever the Council wanted a question answered or needed to collect information, Liev and Milo were dragged down to appear in person. As if they couldn't lie or cheat their way through these sessions in person, like they might through a HoloKomp. He suspected that the Council ran illegal scans on every person who entered these rooms. Hence the reason for keeping Lani out. She might not pass the scans.

He needed the Council to find nothing wrong for a few more months. Then he would start asking them to back off before he involved the lawyers at a more in-depth level. As it was, today was one step from harassment. And Hahn had brought that up more than once. But Liev needed to keep a low profile while Lani settled in. No one could take a closer look at her right now.

He couldn't imagine the shock of what she'd been

put through. He didn't think he'd have handled it half as well as she had if he'd been in the same situation. In fact, he knew he wouldn't. He looked around, seeing Milo and his lawyer, ... his extended family only a call away. He'd lose everything familiar and dear.

Just like Lani had.

For the first time, he had a little insight into all that she'd lost.

And how little he could do to make up for it. He'd done his best to protect her, but he could never replace everything.

"Liev?" Hahn nudged him. With a startled look at his old friend, he realized the Council was talking.

"We need to know any information," the elder Councilman, Carlson, said in a tone that demanded obedience. "Any names or locations that you may have heard Johan mention to track him down."

Liev frowned while he stopped to consider the request. "In truth, I'm not sure I ever heard him mention anyone or any place in particular. He was notorious for his parties, and serious talk didn't happen then, nor were any partygoers willing to engage in serious talk either."

"And yet, he mentioned the two of you going out for coffee after your last appearance here."

Liev's eyebrows shot up at the reminder. However, he answered smoothly, "He did invite me, but the coffee never happened. He wanted to see his lawyers instead, so he asked for a rain check."

That, at least, was the truth. He suspected the Council members already knew what he'd done that day. A drone would have noted his and Johan's actions at the time and would have promptly submitted a report on both men to be filed away for future reference.

The Council muttered among themselves for a long moment. "Your answers have been recorded. Should you have any further information to offer regarding the issue, please contact the office."

A different Council member spoke. "We notice that Milo has not added anything to the conversation."

Liev shrugged. "He has nothing to say. He had nothing to do with Johan."

"Not one of the regular partygoers?" Eyebrows shot sky-high, and amused twitters rippled through the Council members.

Milo was an anomaly to them. He lived in his own world and wouldn't have attended one of Johan's parties if Milo's life had depended on it. Milo's parties were always private with his other geek friends. Liev highly suspected they played more computer games than sex games when they were together. Milo's whole group was more active sexually in VR than in real life.

But that might also be his age or his perspective on other people. Milo was light-years ahead of others. While normal people looked into their coffee cups, wondering at the pretty pattern the cream made as it was poured, Milo had already analyzed its composition, calories, health detriments, and health benefits for everyone in the damn room, as well as who could tolerate that level of fat and who should be running in the opposite direction.

No one was like his brother.

Councilman Carlson said, "And the other occupant in your residence?"

"My wife, Lani?" Liev hated the way Carlson spoke about Lani. "You know her name is Lani. She isn't an occupant." She was so much more, but in their arrogance, they tried to dehumanize her that way.

"Is she here?" The speaker ignored Liev's comment, choosing instead to stare at him in a cold manner.

"She is waiting in the outer chamber." Liev curled his upper lip, his tone even but hard. "I speak on her behalf. All documents have been filed as per protocol."

After a moment where the men clicked away on their comps to verify his statement, the men nodded. Stephen smiled at Liev as they were dismissed.

Liev promptly turned and silently let his breath *whoosh* out. So they'd skated by safely again.

But for how much longer?

He pushed Milo ahead of him as they walked out. Now to collect Lani and to get her home, safe and sound.

As he walked back into the anteroom, she was no longer sitting where he'd left her.

In fact, he saw no sign of her. "Shit."

Book 2 is available now!

To find out more visit Dale Mayer's website.

https://geni.us/DMPajamasUniversal

Arsenic in the Azaleas

A new cozy mystery series from USA Today best-selling author Dale Mayer. Follow gardener and amateur sleuth Doreen Montgomery—and her amusing and mostly lovable cat, dog, and parrot—as they catch murderers and solve crimes in lovely Kelowna, British Columbia.

Riches to rags. ... Controlling to chaos. ... But murder ... seriously?

After her ex-husband leaves her high and dry, former socialite Doreen Montgomery's chance at a new life comes in the form of her grandmother, Nan's, dilapidated old house in picturesque Kelowna ... and the added job of caring for the animals Nan couldn't take into assisted living with her: Thaddeus, the loquacious African gray parrot with a ripe vocabulary, and his buddy, Goliath, a monster-size cat with an equally monstrous attitude.

It's the new start Doreen and her beloved basset hound, Mugs, desperately need. But, just as things start to look up for Doreen, Goliath the cat and Mugs the dog find a human finger in Nan's overrun garden.

And not just a finger. Once the police start digging, the rest of the body turns up and turns out to be connected to an old unsolved crime.

With her grandmother as the prime suspect, Doreen soon finds herself stumbling over clues and getting on Corporal Mack Moreau's last nerve, as she does her best to prove her beloved Nan innocent of murder.

Arsenic in the Azaleas is available now!
To find out more visit Dale Mayer's website.
https://geni.us/DMArsenicUniversal

Author's Note

Thank you for reading Cat's Meow! If you enjoyed my book, I'd appreciate it if you'd leave a review.

Dear reader,

I love to hear from readers, and you can contact me at my website: www.dalemayer.com or at my Facebook author page. To be informed of new releases and special offers, sign up for my newsletter or follow me on BookBub. And if you are interested in joining Dale Mayer's Reader Group, here is the Facebook sign up page.
http://geni.us/DaleMayerFBGroup

Cheers,
Dale Mayer

About the Author

Dale Mayer is a *USA Today* best-selling author, best known for her SEALs military romances, her Psychic Visions series, and her Lovely Lethal Garden cozy series. Her contemporary romances are raw and full of passion and emotion (Broken But ... Mending, Hathaway House series). Her thrillers will keep you guessing (Kate Morgan, By Death series), and her romantic comedies will keep you giggling (*It's a Dog's Life*, a stand-alone novella; and the Broken Protocols series, starring Charming Marvin, the cat).

Dale honors the stories that come to her—and some of them are crazy, break all the rules and cross multiple genres!

To go with her fiction, she also writes nonfiction in many different fields, with books available on résumé writing, companion gardening, and the US mortgage system. All her books are available in print and ebook format.

Connect with Dale Mayer Online

Dale's Website – www.dalemayer.com
Twitter – @DaleMayer
Facebook Page – geni.us/DaleMayerFBFanPage
Facebook Group – geni.us/DaleMayerFBGroup
BookBub – geni.us/DaleMayerBookbub
Instagram – geni.us/DaleMayerInstagram
Goodreads – geni.us/DaleMayerGoodreads
Newsletter – geni.us/DaleNews

Also by Dale Mayer

Published Adult Books:

Hathaway House
Aaron, Book 1

Brock, Book 2

Cole, Book 3

Denton, Book 4

Elliot, Book 5

Finn, Book 6

Gregory, Book 7

Heath, Book 8

Iain, Book 9

Jaden, Book 10

Keith, Book 11

The K9 Files
Ethan, Book 1

Pierce, Book 2

Zane, Book 3

Blaze, Book 4

Lucas, Book 5

Parker, Book 6

Carter, Book 7

Weston, Book 8

Lovely Lethal Gardens

Arsenic in the Azaleas, Book 1

Bones in the Begonias, Book 2

Corpse in the Carnations, Book 3

Daggers in the Dahlias, Book 4

Evidence in the Echinacea, Book 5

Footprints in the Ferns, Book 6

Gun in the Gardenias, Book 7

Handcuffs in the Heather, Book 8

Ice Pick in the Ivy, Book 9

Psychic Vision Series

Tuesday's Child

Hide 'n Go Seek

Maddy's Floor

Garden of Sorrow

Knock Knock...

Rare Find

Eyes to the Soul

Now You See Her

Shattered

Into the Abyss

Seeds of Malice

Eye of the Falcon

Itsy-Bitsy Spider

Unmasked

Deep Beneath

From the Ashes

Stroke of Death

Psychic Visions Books 1–3

Psychic Visions Books 4–6

Psychic Visions Books 7–9

By Death Series

Touched by Death

Haunted by Death

Chilled by Death

By Death Books 1–3

Broken Protocols – Romantic Comedy Series

Cat's Meow

Cat's Pajamas

Cat's Cradle

Cat's Claus

Broken Protocols 1-4

Broken and... Mending

Skin

Scars

Scales (of Justice)

Broken but... Mending 1-3

Glory

Genesis

Tori

Celeste

Glory Trilogy

Biker Blues

Morgan: Biker Blues, Volume 1

Cash: Biker Blues, Volume 2

SEALs of Honor

Mason: SEALs of Honor, Book 1

Hawk: SEALs of Honor, Book 2

Dane: SEALs of Honor, Book 3

Swede: SEALs of Honor, Book 4

Shadow: SEALs of Honor, Book 5

Cooper: SEALs of Honor, Book 6

Markus: SEALs of Honor, Book 7

Evan: SEALs of Honor, Book 8

Mason's Wish: SEALs of Honor

Chase: SEALs of Honor, Book 9

Brett: SEALs of Honor, Book 10

Devlin: SEALs of Honor, Book 11

Easton: SEALs of Honor, Book 12

Ryder: SEALs of Honor, Book 13

Macklin: SEALs of Honor, Book 14

Corey: SEALs of Honor, Book 15

Warrick: SEALs of Honor, Book 16

Tanner: SEALs of Honor, Book 17

Jackson: SEALs of Honor, Book 18

Kanen: SEALs of Honor, Book 19

Nelson: SEALs of Honor, Book 20

Taylor: SEALs of Honor, Book 21

Colton: SEALs of Honor, Book 22

Troy: SEALs of Honor, Book 23

SEALs of Honor, Books 1–3

SEALs of Honor, Books 4–6

SEALs of Honor, Books 7–9

SEALs of Honor, Books 10–12

SEALs of Honor, Books 13–15

SEALs of Honor, Books 16–18

Heroes for Hire

Levi's Legend: Heroes for Hire, Book 1

Stone's Surrender: Heroes for Hire, Book 2

Merk's Mistake: Heroes for Hire, Book 3

Rhodes's Reward: Heroes for Hire, Book 4

Flynn's Firecracker: Heroes for Hire, Book 5

Logan's Light: Heroes for Hire, Book 6

Harrison's Heart: Heroes for Hire, Book 7

Saul's Sweetheart: Heroes for Hire, Book 8

Dakota's Delight: Heroes for Hire, Book 9

Michael's Mercy (Part of Sleeper SEAL Series)

Tyson's Treasure: Heroes for Hire, Book 10

SEALs of Steel

SEALs of Steel, Books 5–8
SEALs of Steel, Books 1–8

The Mavericks
Kerrick, Book 1
Griffin, Book 2
Jax, Book 3
Beau, Book 4
Asher, Book 5
Ryker, Book 6
Miles, Book 7
Nico, Book 8
Keane, Book 9
Lennox, Book 10
Gavin, Book 11
Shane, Book 12

Bullard's Battle Series
Ryland's Reach, Book 1
Cain's Cross, Book 2
Eton's Escape, Book 3
Garret's Gambit, Book 4
Kano's Keep, Book 5
Fallon's Flaw, Book 6
Quinn's Quest, Book 7
Bullard's Beauty, Book 8

Collections
Dare to Be You...
Dare to Love...
Dare to be Strong...
RomanceX3

Standalone Novellas
It's a Dog's Life
Riana's Revenge
Second Chances

Published Young Adult Books:

Family Blood Ties Series
Vampire in Denial
Vampire in Distress
Vampire in Design
Vampire in Deceit
Vampire in Defiance
Vampire in Conflict
Vampire in Chaos
Vampire in Crisis
Vampire in Control
Vampire in Charge
Family Blood Ties Set 1–3
Family Blood Ties Set 1–5
Family Blood Ties Set 4–6

Family Blood Ties Set 7–9

Sian's Solution, A Family Blood Ties Series Prequel
Novelette

Design series

Dangerous Designs

Deadly Designs

Darkest Designs

Design Series Trilogy

Standalone

In Cassie's Corner

Gem Stone (a Gemma Stone Mystery)

Time Thieves

Published Non-Fiction Books:

Career Essentials

Career Essentials: The Résumé

Career Essentials: The Cover Letter

Career Essentials: The Interview

Career Essentials: 3 in 1

9 781773 363851